GUNS OF DRAGONARD

Rupert Gilchrist

SOUVENIR PRESS

ISBN 0 285 62453 9

Printed in Great Britain by
Bristol Typesetting Co. Ltd,
Barton Manor, St. Philips, Bristol

CONTENTS

DRAGONARD
FAMILIES
1778–1864

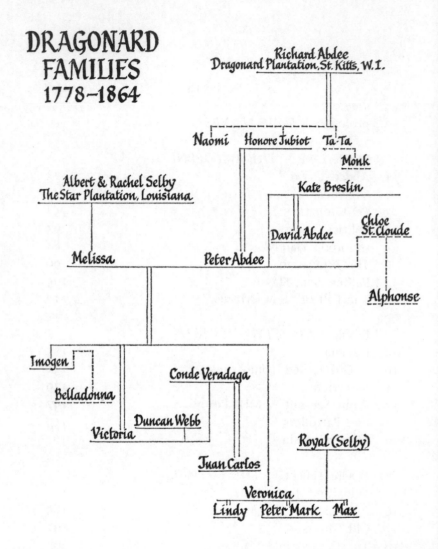

Richard Abdee
Dragonard Plantation, St. Kitts, W.I.

Naomi   Honore Jubiot   Ta-Ta

Monk

Albert & Rachel Selby
The Star Plantation, Louisiana

Kate Breslin

David Abdee

Chloe
St. Cloude

Melissa   Peter Abdee

Alphonse

Imogen

Belladonna

Conde Veradaga

Duncan Webb

Victoria

Juan Carlos

Royal (Selby)

Veronica

Lindy   Peter Mark   Max

prologue

LOVE SLAVES

Greenleaf Plantation,
Louisiana
1861

Tim trudged along a narrow forest path with five other
young Negroes on a Sunday afternoon – the one day
of the week when plantation slaves could strip off their
tow work clothing and spend time as they pleased.

The Louisiana summer heat was cloying; Tim and his
five virile friends were headed for a swimming pool –
The Pothole – located near the eastern perimeter of
Greenleaf Plantation; they had already removed their
shirts and unknotted the ropes tied around their baggy
trousers, anxious to dive into the icy cold water and
wash the dust of the field from their bodies, to splash
and play rough-and-tumble games in The Pothole and,
then, after their swim, they would lie naked in the sun.

Greenleaf Plantation was owned by Peter Abdee who
lived nearby on Dragonard Hill Plantation; Abdee had
long-ago placed Tim's parents in charge of Greenleaf
where they lived comfortably in the plantation's big
house, sharing it only with Alphonse St Cloude, the
illegitimate son of Abdee and a free Negress named Chloe
St Cloude; Tim lived in a dormitory with other field
slaves.

As the small group of young black men walked single
file along the forest path, a burly nineteen-year-old
Negro named Sebbie called to Tim at the front of the
line, 'How's your Ma putting up with fancy pants
Alphonse St Cloude since Miss Chloe high-tailed it to
Dragonard Hill to shack up with Master Peter?' Chloe

St Cloude now lived openly as Peter Abdee's mistress.

'Yeah,' called a burr-headed young man named Franklin. 'What does your Pa say about Alphonse putting on airs he picks up on those visits to New Orleans?'

Tim did not like to repeat stories his parents told him; Maybelle and Ham had emphatically cautioned Tim that a slave's role was to be a servant and not a critic.

He answered, 'Ma and Pa says Master Alphonse will soon be getting over his uppitty ways.'

' "Master" Alphonse?' Franklin let out a whoop. 'Why in hell you call that coon "master"? Alphonse St Cloude's got black blood in his veins same as all us!'

'Maybe Alphonse gots him a drop or two of black blood,' Tim said as he ambled along the dirt path winding through the pine forest, 'but he still ain't no slave like us. He was born a free man. Sired by Master Peter out of a octoroon filly. Alphonse's skin so light he can nearly pass for a white buck.'

'Passing for a white buck is one thing,' quipped Sebbie, 'but being white is another. No matter how light-skinned that Alphonse dandy thinks he is, the bastard's still nigger same as you and me.'

Jonah called from the end of the line. 'Hey, Tim! You're friend of Master Peter's son, David. He's a bona fide white man and heir to both plantations. What does David Abdee say about that Alphonse St Cloude trying to act so fancy? Getting dressed up in silk shirts and tall leather boots? Riding a chestnut stallion to New Orleans like some big shot planter's son? Gambling silver money and drinking wine out of glasses?'

Tim was the same age as David Abdee; they were both thirty-one years old and both unmarried. Tim and David Abdee had spent their childhood together as playmates at Greenleaf but, as David's frail health had degenerated following his own mother's untimely death – and after Tim had been sent to work as a field slave – their friendship had quickly faded.

Sebbie called before Tim had time to reply, 'I hears Alphonse is so greedy he can't wait for David Abdee to die. I hear that Alphonse has plans to be Master Peter's heir. Is that right, Tim? Does us niggers has to start worrying about David Abdee dying some day soon and Alphonse St Cloude becoming master over us?'

Tim mumbled, 'I don't know nothing about life at Dragonard Hill. David Abdee and me, sure we used to be friends. But that was when we were just kids. Since Master David's grown up and took more sickly, we don't see much of each other no more.'

'I hear David Abdee's an abolitionist,' called the Negro named Bullshot. 'That he reads a lot of Yankee books and believes black folks ain't to be kept as white masters' slaves. People say that David Abdee believes just like his sister up north.'

'Sister up north?' asked Sebbie. 'Is that Master Peter's daughter who married a house nigger from Dragonard Hill and hasn't been back down home here since her step-ma was thrown from that horse?'

Tim did not like the direction which the conversation was taking. He said with authority, 'The Abdee family has been good to all of us. To us folks here on Greenleaf and to his other people over on Dragonard Hill. We got no reason to gossip like old ladies about what's none of our business.'

'Things are changing, Tim,' said the black man walking directly behind him. 'You've heard talk about that nigger, John Brown, ain't you? How John Brown got guns, marched on Harper's Landing, and then got hanged just a few months ago?'

'Sure I heard talk about John Brown. But I ain't stupid like you to go gabbing about it. The white folks hanged John Brown, didn't they? The white folks proved once again that a nigger who gets guns gets killed himself. And not you. Not me. Not John Brown. Not nobody is never going to let a nigger get near a gun for as long as he lives.'

The Harper's Landing incident had left bitterness even in peace-loving people like Tim, the son of Maybelle and Ham to whom Peter Abdee had entrusted Greenleaf Plantation.

*　　　*　　　*

Tim, Franklin, Sebbie and the other three young black men emerged hungry from their swim in The Pothole; Tim unwrapped cold pieces of fried chicken, raw turnip wedges and slices of buttered bread which his mother had wrapped in a cheesecloth bundle for the young men to enjoy on their Sunday outing. When the small picnic was finished, the young men sprawled naked in the sun and began to exchange stories.

Bullshot, the most huskily built of the six field slaves, lounged on a grassy incline. The sun caught the drops of water laced like diamonds through the black pubic hairs tightly curled in his crotch and armpits as he lay with both hands locked behind his head.

He mused, 'I always wanted to lays still like I am now. I always wanted to lays dead still and have some wench squatting naked over my pecker. To have some little black gal doing all the work on my pecker while I just lays back smiling and watching her titties bounce up and down.'

Sebbie grunted nearby, 'Sounds pretty good to me. Sounds real good having some gal working her wet little pussy to get hold of my pecker and working it hard for me. That would make her my love slave.'

Franklin toyed with his limp penis as he listened, not squeezing to work his bulky masculinity into an erection, merely tossing his full-crowned brown phallus back and forth from side to side, agreeing, 'Yep, that kind of slavery sounds real pleasing. Love slavery.'

The sinewy Negro named Jonah boasted alongside Franklin. 'I just had me that kind of slavery last week. I has me that gal, Shira, from the looming house. She worked that wet pussy of hers on my pecker till I has me not one drop of spunk left inside me. I can still feel Shira's greedy hole pumping away on my pecker.'

'Shira? Hell, I've has that Shira!' bragged Franklin. 'Shira's game for anything. But I can't rightly say she's ever done the squats on me. Shira mostly sucks on me with her mouth. Says she's spooked of getting knocked up and being put in the birthing shed. Good suck job. Dang good! Shira's good any which way at playing love slave to a good master man.'

Jonah said, 'I wouldn't mind being master man now. Have me some gal like Shira curled right down here between these two legs of mine. Making her first suck my balls. Telling her to squeeze both balls into her mouth. Then ordering her to slick up my pecker with her spit real good.'

'Sounds tempting,' Franklin murmured, still tossing his limp penis back and forth with one hand. 'Sounds right tempting to be bossing some love slave gal to gets me longer . . . thicker . . . harder . . .'

'Harder?' Sebbie bolted up from the ground asking 'You hard, man?'

Franklin dropped both hands to his sides and thrust his groin upwards. 'Hard? Me hard just *talking* about poontang? Hells no, nigger!'

'Jonah?' Sebbie looked to the other side of him. 'You hard?'

'From this jabber? Shit, no!'

Sebbie next sprang to his knees and pointed at the young black boy, Billy, who had joined them for the first time today. Sebbie jubilantly called, 'But Billy's hard! Look, you horny niggers! Look at little Billy there! Hard as a poker!'

Billy moved both hands quickly to hide the firm erection which the older Negroes' talk had aroused on him. But Billy did not move quickly enough. Jonah, Sebbie, Franklin and Bullshot surrounded him, grabbing his arms and legs.

'The water!' Sebbie shouted, ready again to start playing games. 'Let's cool Billy down in the water! Let's shrink that boner back into that skin hood he dangles over his pecker!'

Tim grinned as he watched Billy struggling to resist the playful men. But a sound suddenly distracted him. He looked overhead and spotted a flock of starlings fly through the treetops.

'Hey, shhh!' Tim whispered, wondering what had made the birds take sudden flight from the tall pine spires. 'Something's coming through the brush! Grab your clothes!'

The men stopped; they held Billy in mid-air as they stared at Tim.

But Tim was already stepping into his tow-trousers, anxiously whispering, 'Listen! I hear brush crackling. Twigs breaking. Sounds like horses coming through the woods.''

The young black men quickly abandoned their play and, following Tim's orders, they grabbed their clothes and removed all traces of the frugal picnic from the grassy slope.

Tim remained in command, ordering his friends to arm themselves with large stones or strong branches, to hide behind the granite boulders beyond the far side of The Pothole, to be prepared if anyone was coming to cause trouble for them.

Bullshot whispered, 'Could be Patrollers.'

'Or poachers from Carterville,' suggested Sebbie.

Tim remembered the incident at Harper's Landing and whispered, 'Or could be some kind of soldiers.'

He moved his hand now for everyone to fall silent as the distinct sound of horses approached through the pine forest.

*   *   *

'Soldiers all right,' Tim whispered, spotting a swarthy man wearing a dark blue hat and his uniform unbuttoned to the waist.

'What kind of soldiers?' whispered Bullshot.

Tim shrugged; he knew nothing about armies; he thought about the Negro, John Brown, who was rapidly becoming a folk hero amongst the slave population, and about Negroes being kept defenceless without guns.

The swarthy white man in the navy blue military hat led a black mare into the opening, the first horse of a pack train, which swayed under a heavy weight covered with tarpaulins.

It was not until the third horse of the pack train came into clear view that Tim and his friends saw wooden stocks of muskets protruding between the pack ropes which secured the tarpaulins onto the weary horses.

'Guns!' whispered Bullshot.

'They sure in hell ain't Patrollers,' Tim said, craning his neck to see how many more soldiers were escorting the pack train.

'Where they be taking guns around here?' asked Sebbie.

Tim did not answer. He was thinking again about Harper's Landing, about how white people had lynched the Negro leader, John Brown, as an example for other black people who wanted their freedom, how everyone said that a Negro would never again be allowed to grip a gun in his hand.

He whispered, 'I counts five soldiers. They look pretty beat. Do you think we can take them?'

'What you saying, Tim?' whispered Sebbie.

Again, Tim did not answer. He knew his friends well. He knew they would follow him in whatever decision he made, whether it be in a field gang or after work when they only had themselves to think about, that not one of them would contest his command to seize an opportunity to secure weapons, strengths, perhaps even self-respect.

Tim's sudden call for attack was a loud shriek; he was the first to jump from the top of the granite boulder, club in hand, and fall on top of the unsuspecting soldier in the navy blue hat. Bullshot, Franklin, Jonah, Sebbie and Billy followed his example, attacking the remaining four soldiers with large stones and clubs.

Amidst the whinnying of the horses, the six Negro slaves pummelled the five unarmed soldiers with the crude weapons they gripped. They did not question Tim about his decision, only vying with one another for courage and strength, deftness of blows.

Blood soon smeared sharp edges of rocks. Black hands gripped white necks. Mahogany strong fists drove against white faces. Thick branches clubbed the soldiers' skulls into unrecognizable pulp. The ambush was quick, complete, total slaughter.

Tim hurried to get the horses under control while

his friends made certain no life was left in any of the soldiers' bodies. He heard Bullshot ordering the others, 'Get rid of these white men. Don't leave no trace of nothing.'

While Sebbie, Franklin, Jonah and Billy followed Bullshot's orders, Tim began making a thorough inspection of the pack train. His calmness surprised himself.

He threw back the tarpaulins, calling, 'Guns all right. More guns than any nigger could hope for. And ammunition. Powder. Balls. Everything niggers needs to be strong.'

Billy, the youngest in the group, was the only one to hesitate. He asked, 'Why we do this, Tim? These white men didn't do us no harm? Why we kill them? What we need guns for?'

'You just keep remembering you're nothing but a nigger slave, boy, and keep your damned mouth shut. Understand?'

The bitterness in Tim's voice sounded alien even to himself; he had not discovered until this cloying summer afternoon in 1861 that every Negro slave possessed a desire for freedom despite how good his master was, regardless what price he might have to pay; that he could fantasize about 'love slaves' but that the only slavery he knew was the slavery into which he – or she – had been born: slavery to white people for life. Tim discovered on this summer afternoon that a desire for rebellion lay dormant in Negroes until an opportunity for sudden power presented itself and, then, he – they – would act impulsively, would murder, would finally see how defenceless Negroes truly were in the American world of masters and slaves.

Book One

THE WILDERNESS

Chapter One

ABDEE BLOOD

D avid Abdee sat again this summer's night, alongside a cluttered table in his bedroom at Dragonard Hill, leaning toward a pewter candelabra to catch the candles' yellow glow for reading before he retired to his bed.

Books were heaped amongst daguerreotypes, dried flowers, brass statuary on the table; more books set in teetering piles on the Oriental carpets layered on the floor and lined endless rows of mahogany shelves, making David Abdee's retreat look more like a library than his bedroom.

Books provided an escape for David Abdee. Biographies. Essays. Poetry. Novels. Romances distracted him from the day-to-day drudgery of plantation life. Histories were more captivating to him than the politics he heard neighbours discussing when they came to visit his father. Atlases and geographies told him that there was a civilized world beyond Dragonard Hill, a world where people talked about subjects other than crops, livestock – and slavery.

Finally closing a small Moroccan bound volume, David slumped back in his chair and rubbed the bridge of his thin nose. He was tired. Fatigued. But not spent from physical labour nor exhausted from exercise. David seldom stepped out of the house, seldom ventured into the fields, nor visited the slave quarters on Dragonard Hill. Although doctors argued about his illness, David suspected that he merely suffered from malaise. Boredom. That he was thirty-one years old and already tired of life.

'Where am I headed?' he asked himself as he sat with his narrow shoulders slumped forward in the chair. 'I talk to no-one. I hide here in my room. Am I frightened of what I will find in the outside world, a world which is fighting a war, a war we keep from our slaves, a war we try to ignore ourselves?

'What if there *is* a war! And what am I doing?'

David's palms moistened with nervous perspiration at the thought of the battle between the northern and southern states over the issue of slavery. He could not envisage himself serving as a soldier.

A distant galloping disturbed David Abdee's tormented thoughts; he glanced toward a small gilt clock on the cluttered table and saw that the time was past nine o'clock, a late hour for a visitor to come calling at Dragonard Hill.

Taking a deep sigh, David marked the page in the Dumas novel with a silk ribbon and arose from the chair to see who was galloping up the driveway from the public road.

David stood alongside the tall window in his quilted dressing-gown, gripping onto the heavy tasselled damask draperies and looked out into the darkness, squinting down at the gravel driveway which circled in front of Dragonard Hill. He saw no rider halting by the six white pillars which fronted the large neo-classical house but, hearing voices, he looked toward the stables. He then saw the black groom, Walter, greeting the late-night caller dismounting from a chestnut stallion.

'Alphonse St Cloude! What is that . . . bastard doing here this late at night? And this is the third time he's been here this week!'

David stood in the window and watched Alphonse

St Cloude snatch the bull's eye lantern from the groom. Alphonse was fastidiously dressed in tight breeches, black leather boots and a coat which was much too elaborately tailored – too foppish – for David's taste.

'Why doesn't Alphonse stay at Greenleaf where he belongs? Or go to New Orleans and never come back?'

David stood by the window, looking down at Alphonse St Cloude disappear around the side of the house with the lantern. David seldom felt proprietorial about Dragonard Hill but, lately, Alphonse St Cloude's visits were becoming far too frequent, were beginning to become annoying and even created anger in David.

David suspected that his father and Chloe had already dined together and were now sitting in the parlour. He wondered, 'Dare I confront father now about Alphonse? Make a scene in front of Chloe? Alphonse must have come to see her. Can I really face him?'

David was halfway to the bedroom door before he thought of his own appearance, that he was attired only in his pyjamas and dressing-gown.

'Who cares?' he asked himself, catching his reflection in a tall cheval mirror. He ran one hand through his black hair prematurely touched with silver and threw open the bedroom door. He knew that if he did not have a serious discussion tonight with his father about Alphonse St Cloude, he might lose his only retreat from the world – one small room in the large house called Dragonard Hill.

*   *   *

David Abdee found his father sitting alone alongside the white Carrara marble fireplace in the parlour; Peter Abdee was sipping brandy by the fire, the glow illuminating his strong-featured face weathered by the sun

25

and the wind, making him look handsome in his maturity, serene – even contemplative – by the fireside, but not a man old enough to be a grandfather.

'David!' Peter Abdee glanced with surprise at his son standing in the half-open door. 'I thought you'd gone to sleep.'

'I was reading,' David curtly answered, sliding the door shut behind him. 'Where's Chloe?'

'Did you want to see her?'

'No, I actually wanted to talk to you. Alone.'

'No better time,' Peter generously said, then asked, 'Brandy?'

David shook his head. He was relieved not to find Alphonse here either.

'Brandy's good medicine,' Peter leaned toward a decanter to splash more of the golden imported liquor into his crystal balloon.

'I don't need medicine.'

Peter resettled himself in the chair and, nodding toward the chair across from him, he said, 'Then call it a night-cap.'

David remained standing; he felt nervous perspiration run down the sides of his chest and hated himself for being cowardly. But he forced himself to be aggressive, saying, 'I don't need a nightcap either, Father. I need serenity. Peace of mind. Reassurance about what's going to happen in the future. Does Alphonse plan to start living here or not?'

Peter Abdee looked up at his son. 'Alphonse?'

'I just saw him ride up the driveway. He's here again tonight. This is the third time this week.'

Swishing the brandy in the crystal balloon, Peter calmly answered, 'He's probably just visiting his mother.'

David asked sarcastically, 'Is it Chloe who extends the hospitality to him? Invites him here?'

26

'David,' Peter began, recrossing his black boots on the silk ottoman in front of him. 'I'm not asking you and Alphonse to be friends. Nor do I ask you to approve of Chloe. But I try to understand you and I wish you would be more understanding of me.'

'This has nothing to do with you and Chloe. Not how Chloe lives with you, your relationship with her. It's him. Your son from Chloe. I think we've all been evading a very important issue for too long, Father. There is the matter of coloured blood, illegitimate offspring and – '

Peter interrupted, 'David, please. Sit down. I want to talk to you about coloured blood. Black people. Slavery – ' he paused, adding ' – and white people.'

'You and I are the only white people left here and on Greenleaf, Father.'

'Are you frightened?'

'Of the slaves?' David answered without considering the question. 'No. I grew up with black people. But I did not grow up with Alphonse St Cloude. He came into my life when I was barely out of my childhood. His mother came to tutor me and then she became your . . . lover.'

'Are you jealous of Alphonse?'

'Of Alphonse? How do you mean, Father?'

Peter said, 'For one thing Alphonse has a mother. I live with her. I have not married her but, yes, she became my lover after your mother died.'

David dug his fists deep into the pockets of his satin dressing-gown, saying, 'I barely remember my own mother. She was killed when I was seven. How could I possibly be jealous of you and Chloe? I say that honestly, too, Father. How could I be jealous? My mother was your second wife. If anybody should be jealous, I suppose it should be the children from your first wife. The heirs – ' David stopped.

27

Peter Abdee had sired three children before David's birth, three daughters born from his first wife, Melissa; Veronica and Victoria Abdee were twins from Peter Abdee's first wife; Veronica was married to a Negro and now lived in Boston; Victoria had repeatedly run away from home with profligate men and her name was never mentioned; Imogen had been the eldest of Peter and Melissa Abdee's daughters and had lived an openly perverse life on Dragonard Hill with a Negress lover until her brutal murder by outraged white neighbours. David Abdee stopped before he mentioned any of his step-sisters' names to his father; he never knew how to broach the subject of them.

Peter abruptly asked, 'Could you accept the fact of me marrying Chloe?'

David, lowering his head, answered, 'What do I know of marriage or love? I could only speak to you on that subject in terms of our neighbours' reactions. The Abdees have upset other white families before.'

'You and I have never been close, David. But if there is anything you want to ask me, please feel free.'

'Ask you about what? The birds and the bees? The facts of life? No,' David said, his thin lips lifting into a smile. 'I learned about the birds and the bees long ago. From Tim. On Greenleaf.' He thought of how Tim had first introduced him to sex, of them both straddling a young Negress who had known more about sex at that time than either of them, of the girl greasing herself with goose fat for Tim to penetrate her with his prematurely large penis and then coaching David to slow his strokes to avoid ejaculating too soon.

'Tim,' Peter repeated, thinking fondly of what a fine young man Maybelle and Ham's son had grown into. He asked, 'Have you seen Tim lately?'

David shrugged, 'I seldom go to Greenleaf, do I?'

28

'Is that because of Alphonse?'

'Partially. And partially because Tim is a slave. He works in the fields. I do not work. Maturity and circumstances have separated us. What once was a friendship between us can not now even be a memory. White gentlemen are not meant to remember the "piccaninnies" they played with as children.'

'David, are you ashamed?' The question was blunt.

'Ashamed?'

Peter recrossed his legs, saying, 'Let me rephrase that. Do you want to be different and don't know how to come to terms with it?'

'Be different? But I *am* different. That's the problem! I am *too* different!'

'Do you want us to talk about that?' Peter was trying to be patient. David had always been a recluse, even as a small boy. But, then, Peter constantly reminded himself that his son had ample reason to remain aloof from the world. What young man would want to fraternize with neighbours who had pegged his step-sister, Imogen, to the ground and then fired a squirrel gun into her vagina? It had been that fateful night at Dragonard Hill when Peter Abdee had sent his son to live at Greenleaf, hoping to cleanse his mind of the hideous spectacle.

'I want us to talk about something, Father,' David fretfully announced, beginning to pace the parlour. 'I want us to talk about many things, Father. There's a barrier between us. I don't know if it's our conflicting viewpoints or Chloe. An age difference between us. But – '

Peter was impressed that David was trying to formulate problems into words, enigmas which had puzzled him when David had failed over the years to adjust to plantation life. He now tried to help. 'David, I've never urged you to travel, to visit New Orleans or Veronica in Boston. Not even to take the buggy into Carterville or Troy.'

Shaking his head, Peter confessed, 'I personally believe, David, it is not healthy for you to stay locked in your room.'

David stood with his back to his father and, without turning around, he asked, 'Will the war continue, Father?'

'War?' The suddenness of the question stunned Peter.

'The Southern states have seceded from the Union. We fired on Fort Sumter in April. Will it spread? Will the slaves revolt on the plantations?'

'People have talked about revolutions and rebellions for years, David.' Peter Abdee took another sip of brandy. The subject of war annoyed him. He had been fighting other, more bigoted battles for years.

'But will the war between the northern and southern states become worse?'

'Let me ask you this, David, do you think of yourself as a loyal southerner?'

'No more than you.'

Peter grunted, then admitted, 'You have obviously been more observant of my activities than I have given you credit for, David. Yes, I'm also somewhat of a misfit in this part of the world. I'm a loner myself. You come by it naturally, I guess.'

'I'm sorry to trouble you with my worries, Father,' David said, turning to the door. 'I should know by now that I must learn to sort out my own problems. To adjust to my own view of the world and answer my own questions. That's the only way a man can discover his abilities.'

'Son?'

David hesitated by the sliding mahogany doors which opened onto the foyer.

'Son, do you realize that this is the first time I've ever heard you refer to yourself as a man?'

David held his father's eyes, saying, 'Is that why this is the first time you've ever called me "son"?'

Reaching for one door, David said, 'I think we better start synchronizing our relationship, Father, if Dragonard Hill is going to stay in the family.'

The mahogany door slid shut behind David; he did not remain to explain his words, but Peter Abdee understood.

*   *   *

Chloe St Cloude, tawny-skinned with jet black hair pulled tightly into a knot at the nape of her neck, sat alongside a pinewood table at that same late hour in the kitchen annex of Dragonard Hill; she slowly read the awkward words printed in ink on thick vellum pages of a letter and ignored the black person – Posey – sitting anxiously beside her.

Posey was as much of a fixture at Dragonard Hill as the six Doric columns fronting the large white mansion referred to as the plantation's 'new house.' Posey had moved many years ago from the 'old house' as a kitchen helper to the former cook, an imperious Negress called Storky; Posey had come not only to assume Storky's role in the passing years but had also gradually assimilated the now deceased Negress's manner of dressing: Posey was a male but dressed in woman's clothing, insisting upon being treated by the lower echelons of black slaves with the same respect paid to his female predecessor.

'Is my word writing okay, Miss Chloe?' Posey asked

eagerly, looking over Chloe St Cloude's shoulder. 'Can you reads the letter I writes?'

Chloe held up one slim hand for Posey to remain silent; she turned another page of the letter and continued to read.

'I know my spelling ain't good – ' Posey began.

'Shush, Miss Posey,' Chloe said, using the same title with which everyone on Dragonard Hill now addressed the androgynous cook.

Posey twitched nervously in his chair; he smoothed the starched white apron covering his long skirt; he tucked at the linen kerchief tied around his head. Chloe St Cloude had not only taught him how to read and write but had also recently suggested writing a letter to Peter Abdee's daughter, Veronica, who lived in Boston with her Negro husband, Royal Selby and their three half-caste children, telling them about life on Dragonard Hill.

Finally, taking a deep sigh, Chloe finished the letter and began folding the crisp pages.

Posey asked, 'Is it awful? Is my letter bad as can be?'

'Miss Posey,' Chloe answered, reaching for Posey's long, slender brown hand, 'your letter is . . . beautiful. Much better than anything I could ever write to Veronica.'

'Oh, no, Miss Chloe!' Posey immediately protested. 'You be a governess! You be the smartest lady in the world!'

Chloe looked lovingly at Posey's angular face, a flat nose spread with brown freckles, features which were neither masculine nor feminine. She said, 'You are almost a member of the Abdee family, Miss Posey. You know more about the Abdees than anyone alive.'

Posey squirmed nervously in his chair, mumbling, 'I had Miss Storky for my first teacher, Miss Chloe. I been around here for many a year. I remember when this place was owned by the Selby family and called "The Star". The Selbys ain't exactly family no more but Master Peter, he married Melissa Selby and she gives him his three daughters. Then he married Mattie Kate who bore him Master David before that rambunctious horse done threw her to her death. I tries to write to Miss Veronica everything I thinks she wants to hear about her daddy and all. Lots of things happen at Dragonard Hill, Miss Chloe. Lots of things always did happen here. They always will. But I chose only to write the good things to Miss Veronica and her family. Miss Veronica suffered a whole lot of badness on her last visit home. I reckons that's why Miss Veronica don't come here no more in all these years. But I knows how she loves this place. I know she especially loves the old house where she was born.'

'The old house! You write such little beautiful things about that tumbled-down old place, Miss Posey. The creaky front porch. The rope swings. The streams out behind it. Every cornflower, jasmine shrub, cypress tree.'

'Miss Veronica, she likes those things. But it don't sound too silly to be writing in a letter? Stuff about that old house?' Posey dipped his head, continuing. 'I can't write too much about other things, Miss Chloe. Lots of news ain't proper for niggers to know. Even if I now be head house nigger here at Dragonard Hill.'

Rising from her chair, Chloe clutched the thick letter in front of her paisley shawl, saying, 'If I never do another thing in my life, Miss Posey, I have at least accomplished one thing! I have taught *you* how to write. I know, I just know that future generations of Abdees will have you to thank for their heritage.'

'Then you likes it? You likes my letter?' Posey's eyes beamed at the petite octoroon woman.

'Yes, Miss Posey. I like it very, very much. And I know Master Abdee will be very impressed.' Chloe paused, eyeing Posey as she softly asked, 'You don't mind if I show your letter to Mister Abdee before I take it to the mail pouch in Carterville?'

'Master Peter?' Posey gasped. 'Master Peter reads what I writes to Miss Veronica? Oh, no, Miss Chloe! Never! Oh, please don't let Master Peter reads my letter!'

'Then what about Master David? He, more than anybody else, would be so proud of you writing such a tender letter to Veronica.'

Posey considered the idea of David Abdee reading his letter. Posey felt a strange connection with David Abdee. Although David was white and Posey was a black slave, they were both house creatures, both hesitant to venture into the outside world.

But the idea of anyone except Veronica and Miss Chloe reading the letter definitely did not appeal to Posey. He stood up from his chair and, taking the thick letter from Chloe's hand, he said, 'Thank you, Miss Chloe. I'm proud to sees you can reads my writing and likes what you reads. That's enough praise for me.'

A voice outside the kitchen door disturbed them.

Posey quickly stuffed the letter into a pocket of his long white apron as Chloe St Cloude hurried toward the kitchen door. They had both recognized the voice and Posey, too anxious to hide the letter, forgot to ask Miss Chloe one more important question, the matter of local laws forbidding black slaves to read, write, or send letters through the governmental post. Alphonse St Cloude always addled 'Miss Posey.'

*　　*　　*

Chloe St Cloude found her son waiting for her on the flagged breezeway which connected the kitchen annex to the main house. She knew that Alphonse was a striking specimen of manhood, true, but she no longer saw his strong chin, his piercing blue eyes and black hair combed straight back from his forehead as handsome features; Alphonse St Cloude was increasingly beginning to impress Chloe as one of the arrogant young dandies she remembered from New Orleans as a young girl, one of the reckless characters peopling the decadent world she had forsaken to come to the wilderness of northern Louisiana.

She clutched the paisley shawl tightly over her breasts and demanded, 'Alphonse! Why do you come here so late at night?'

'What's the matter, chère maman?' he asked, looking even more rakish than usual as he stood in the moonlight. 'Aren't I good enough to mingle with white folks?'

'Do not use that tone of voice with me.' The sweetness which Chloe had used when speaking to Posey now completely disappeared when she addressed her son.

'What tone shall I use with you, chère maman? The same as when I speak to my father?'

Alphonse paused to mimic the dialect of the plantation slaves, 'Yes, Master Peter. No, Master Peter.'

'Why do you come here at night?' Chloe repeated, her eyes as brilliant as the sapphires and black diamonds mounted on the brooch pinned beneath her thin neck.

'I'm a grown man, chère maman. Also, I am not a slave. I do not need a pass to travel on the public road after dark. Or perhaps you have been living here so long that you've become concerned about the harmful effects of night air on young men! But have no such fears about me! I am strong! Much stronger than Master Peter's other son, that weakling who stays locked in his room with his nose stuck in a book.'

'Shhh,' Chloe said, tugging Alphonse from the breeze-

35

way, pushing him into the shadows behind the kitchen annex. 'Do not talk like that about David.'

'David? Oh, you've become intimate with him, too, I see! You no longer call him "Master David". Gone is the young boy you came from New Orleans to tutor. Now it is "David."'

'I will now ignore this open defiance of me. But if you persist, Alphonse, you will be alone. Totally lost. You have made enemies with practically everyone at Greenleaf and Dragonard Hill. Soon even I will not be able to defend you.'

'Defend me?' Alphonse laughed. 'But chère maman, you abandoned me. You left me at Greenleaf. You moved here to Dragonard Hill and left me alone in a houseful of common . . . niggers!'

'Stop it, Alphonse! For shame! Maybelle and Ham are fine people. Maybelle takes good care of you. She waits on you hand and foot. Her own son lives with field workers in a slave barracks. Tim goes to work at the crack of dawn while you lounge in your bed until noon!'

'You keep forgetting one thing, chère maman. I may have a drop or two of Negro blood in my veins but I am no slave. I have Abdee blood in me. I may be called by your family name but also – like your cherished David – I am an Abdee!'

Alphonse then gripped his mother tightly on her thin wrist, ordering, 'I want you to secure me the use of that name, maman.'

'Are you threatening me, Alphonse? Ordering your mother?'

'I have never asked you for one thing, maman. Did I ask you to come to this God-forsaken part of Louisiana? Did I ask you to become Peter Abdee's mistress? To bear him an illegitimate child? Then to abandon me and move here to the luxuries of Dragonard Hill?'

Alphonse's sharp questions brought tears to Chloe's large brown eyes. She knew her son could be heartless but she had never before suffered such insolence from him.

Loosening his grip on her wrist, Alphonse said in a softer voice, 'Maman, I am only trying to tell you that I have my pride too. Perhaps my pride is even stronger than yours. Do not forget that I have Abdee blood in my veins.'

She flared, 'The Abdees are good people!'

'Good people!' He laughed bitterly. 'Public whip-masters. Slave traders. Whores. That's what the Abdees are.'

Chloe gripped at her shawl, resisting the urge to strike her son across his face, despite how handsome he was.

'You love him, don't you, maman? You love old Peter Abdee?'

'Of course I love him. And what's more, stop calling him "old".'

Alphonse smirked; he knew that Peter Abdee had the virility of a much younger man; he also realized that Peter and his mother enjoyed a highly active sex life. He asked, 'Do you love him more than you love me?'

'Do you think I could give myself to a man I did not love?' Chloe never tried to hide her physical relationship with Peter Abdee, not even from her confessor; she had forsaken her staunch Catholicism for their love.

'You evade my question, maman. Do you love Peter Abdee more than you love me?'

'There can be no comparisons between such loves. But I do not love you where you are disrespectful. When you act like this. Defiant. Hostile. Rude. Determined to cause trouble.'

37

'Oh, I am very capable of causing trouble, maman. And only you can stop me. With those fingers he rings with diamonds. With those wrists he encircles with gold. With that body he dresses in expensive satin. Yes, Maman, you and you alone control my destiny.'

'Me?'

Alphonse's eyes narrowed and, bringing his face closer to his mother's, he hissed, 'You can persuade Peter Abdee to recognize me legally as his heir. You can secure me my . . . patrimony.'

'Alphonse!' she angrily whispered. 'You know such a thing is impossible. You are coloured. Your father is white, yes. But your mother is coloured. A free woman of colour and that makes you coloured too.'

'Free men of colour own businesses in New Orleans, maman. They are respected citizens in that city. And soon free men of colour will own many acres of land. Plantations! Cotton gins! Vast tracts of timber! And I intend to be one of them. I intend to inherit Dragonard Hill!'

Chloe St Cloude reeled at her son so blatantly confessing his ambitions. She warned him, 'You be thankful you have a place to live, Alphonse! You be thankful you have bread on the table and a roof over your head at Greenleaf.'

'We shall see what will make me thankful, maman. We shall see.' Alphonse bowed with mock gallantry, announcing, 'Now, I have other business to tend to, maman. Bonsoir to you and my . . . papa. I trust you shall soon be joining him.'

Chloe St Cloude watched her son striding off into the night towards the stables; she knew his restlessness would cause trouble, but she also knew that he was correct in saying that only she could prevent it.

Alphonse St Cloude did not return to Greenleaf
Plantation when he left his mother but, after collecting
his horse from the stable, he rode to the slave quarters
on Dragonard Hill called 'Town', a small community
of wooden cabins built on stilts, low-pitched dormitories
and a clapboard chapel which was set at the intersection
of two dirt roads. Alphonse had arranged to meet a
young black girl tonight, a young Negress with whom
he could indulge his perverse and often cruel sexual
fantasies.

The slave girl's name was Mavis; Alphonse saw her
waiting at the designated spot in a copse of chinaberry
trees; he slowed his horse before the dirt path opened
onto the crossing where the weathered chapel stood as
a relic of a past era.

Mavis slowly emerged onto the path; Alphonse called
'You horny, gal? You horny waiting for me?'

Mavis looked nervously around her in the shadows;
she knew she would be ostracized by the other black
slaves if she were discovered making love to a free man
of colour. She was taking this chance because Alphonse
was the nearest specimen of white gentry she could
hope to enjoy.

'You going to play with me, gal?'

She looked up at Alphonse sitting like a prince on
horseback totally unlike the black slaves who reeked
of musky perspiration.

Alphonse ordered, 'Hoist that skirt to your belly, gal.
Let me see your pussy. Better yet, let me see you finger
your pussy.'

'I wants to make love with you . . . Master Alphonse.'

Alphonse danced his horse closer to the nervous black

girl; he held his riding crop in one hand, saying, 'Hoist that skirt to your belly, bitch, and start fingering yourself for me.'

Mavis slowly, obediently, lifted the ragged hem of her osnaburgh dress with one hand and, cautiously, she began to move her other hand toward the dark patch between her thin legs.

Alphonse, satisfied with the girl's immediate effort to obey him, leaned back in his saddle and began rubbing the crotch of his breeches. He watched Mavis pet her feminine mound with one hand whilst he himself began to free his own sexuality from his breeches; his phallus hardened as he saw the girl becoming more bold, her middle fingers now clumped together to poke at the moisture patch between her legs.

Alphonse stood in the stirrups of his saddle; he jutted his phallus forward, boasting, 'See this, wench?'

Mavis still worked on herself, stepping closer toward Alphonse to see that his penis was even larger than the usual rod it formed inside his breeches.

Alphonse slapped his growing erection against the leather saddle-horn, demanding, 'Is this what you want poked in your pussy? Is this what you're slobbering for like some poor cow?'

Mavis slunk back at his derisive words; she answered, 'The night's chilly but I know a little empty shack . . .'

'Shut up, nigger! Hear me? Shut up, nigger! Hear that? "Nigger"! I call you "nigger". And that's what you are. "Nigger". Just a nigger. You're lucky to get this look at me! Lucky just to be standing where you are. Why, there are white ladies in New Orleans who would gladly pay a golden eagle to be where you're standing . . . nigger bitch!'

Alphonse then launched into his favourite fantasy,

telling the unsophisticated young slave girl how rich and beautiful white ladies in New Orleans fought for his sexual favours; he sat on his stallion and slapping his iron-hard penis against the saddle-horn, he told Mavis how women sought him out for amorous assignations in the French Quarter and the Garden District of New Orleans.

Finally, Alphonse completely ignored the girl standing near the horse. He became totally involved in his wishful dreams of being the toast of New Orleans society; he worked his fist harder and harder on his penis as he spoke about titled ladies and officers' wives grovelling to be his servant for a night, embellishing his fantasies, feeding his dreams, working his penis and taunting the girl until finally a cascade of sperm jutted forth onto the saddle; he closed his eyes, jerking his groin as the last shots of sperm fell onto the leather.

Alphonse St Cloude only realized that Mavis had moved closer to the horse when he felt her hand cautiously touch his thigh; he immediately kneed her away but, then dipping his fingertips into the white puddles of sperm on the saddle, he held his hand toward her face.

He said, 'You get . . . this'.

Smiling as he watched Mavis greedily, gratefully suck his long fingers, Alphonse mocked her with cruel words, saying, 'Oh, the women of New Orleans who would pay for what you are getting to eat tonight for free, nigger gal! Getting to swallow for free! So you work your other hand in your pussy and think about that while you're eating my cum . . . eat my cum, nigger girl. Eat that cum!'

The newness of speaking about sexuality, rather than actually copulating with a man, excited Mavis and she obediently masturbated herself whilst acting as

Alphonse's subservient partner, thankfully cleaning every trace of seed off his fingers, his knuckles, his fist now digging into her throat as she worked her own hand into the enlargening lips of her furry vagina.

Chapter Two

GREENLEAF

Maybelle, a sturdy Negress with black hair cropped close to her head, had learned long ago to abide by plantation rules which dictated that slave mothers must sever all family ties with their offspring immediately after childbirth. Maybelle had tried to follow such a code. But she could not completely alienate herself from her son, Tim, and considered herself extremely fortunate to have Peter Abdee as a master who was lenient with his slaves.

Maybelle knew that Tim was reluctant to come to the main house at Greenleaf now that he had matured into a man, that he did not want to differentiate himself from his friends in the slave barracks, to be unlike other Negroes because his father was Greenleaf's overseer and his mother lived in the plantation's main house as if she were its white mistress.

Both Maybelle and Ham respected Tim for his attitude but, nonetheless, Maybelle had recently begun to arrange what appeared to be chance meetings with her son; she saw that Tim had matured into a natural leader of men and wanted to ensure that his innate ability of leadership did not get him into trouble. Black leaders, she knew, often were punished – even killed – by white people.

This morning's meeting took place beyond the blacksmithy; Maybelle, knowing that Tim brought scythes to the whetstone there, lingered on her way back to the main house from the chicken coop, hoping to talk to her son alone; she finally saw him trudging from the work houses and smiled with pride at his healthy, strong frame.

She called, 'Your Pa and me ain't seen much of you lately, boy.'

'The crop's ripening.' Tim was never rude to his mother but neither was he overly friendly; his sober demeanour was also clouded since he had led his five friends in the attack on the munitions pack-train and he had buried the guns in a place known only to him; also, his sleep had been disturbed lately by nightmares, by troubling dreams about soldiers screaming as he and his friends slaughtered them for the guns. He was beginning to wonder if the possession of guns was worth his nagging conscience.

'You had time to visit us before,' Maybelle said, repositioning her basket of eggs on one arm. 'Master Abdee ain't strict about rules like other planters be. Or maybe it's Master Alphonse who's keeping you away from the kitchen.'

Tim cast an unfriendly glance toward the yellow-roofed house standing behind his mother.

Maybelle assured him, 'No worry. Alphonse is still sleeping.'

'He ain't bothering you none, Ma, is he? Making you and Pa no trouble?' Tim's voice was deep, as sober as his face.

'Your Mama can take care of herself, boy. I lets Master Alphonse thinks he a real fancy-man. But he knows he can't get away with no turkey-trot with old Maybelle here!' She thumbed the blue cambric dress straining against her ample breasts.

Tim remembered the questions about Alphonse and David Abdee which other slaves had asked him. He

44

studied his mother, saying, 'Do you think Alphonse might move to Dragonard Hill like Miss Chloe?'

'It ain't up to your Pa and me to think about what sassy Master Alphonse is planning. We just do our jobs taking care of Greenleaf for Master Peter, both keeping our mouths shut like good niggers.'

'Ma, there's something – '

Tim stopped. He shook his head. He wanted to confide in his mother about the pack-train of guns, about where he had buried the cache of muskets and ammunition. But his mother's loyalty to Peter Abdee stopped him. He felt the lonely burden of leadership, of having made a decision to murder strangers and the importance of guarding the secret.

Maybelle saw her son's forehead furrow; she said, to put him at ease, 'I know your Pa ain't a talkative man, boy. I also know he don't like to shows you no favours he don't give to other bucks in the field. Not that you'd take favours. But if there's something you've got to talk about, get your Pa alone and ask him. Fact is, boy, your Pa and me were just talking about you ourselves, saying it's way past time you thought of marrying, about jumping the broom with some nice little gal.'

'Marrying, Ma? Finding some gal to settle down with? Or do you just want me to sire my share of piccaninnies for Master Peter? Give him more slaves to work in the field and cotton gin?'

'Tim?' Maybelle asked, cocking her head to one side. 'You turning bitter against Master Peter?'

'No more bitter than any other nigger slaves.' Tim looked his mother in the eye, asking, 'Ma, you heard about that nigger, John Brown, they hanged up at Harper's Landing?'

'Shh, you fool.' Maybelle looked quickly around the dirt yard. 'A body don't know who's eavesdropping.

Don't you ever let me hear you mention that man's name again. You may be tall as a tree but your Ma can still smack you one.'

'How's things in the kitchen?' Tim asked, hoping to wipe the frown from his mother's face, wanting also to lift his own spirits. 'How's Hettie working out for you?'

'Hettie? Why you ask about Hettie for, boy? You can do one heck of a lot better than Hettie! She might works for me in the kitchen but that gal ain't nothing but a barn slut!'

Tim had indeed noticed Hettie's curvaceous body but he knew better than to meet a Negress who worked so closely with his mother. He smiled for the first time, saying, 'You really wants to marry me off, don't you, Ma?'

The sound of a carriage crunching over the gravel driveway beyond a field of quack grass attracted Tim's attention; he glanced towards the poplars lining the driveway which cut through the field and mumbled, 'Time for me to get back to work.'

Maybelle shaded her eyes against the sun, looking towards the poplars, saying, 'It's only Master David, boy. He's come to have lunch with your Pa and me. Why don't you come sits with us for a spell in the kitchen?'

'I got field work to do, Ma.' Tim gripped the scythe handles.

'But Master David likes you, Tim. You used to be good friends. It ain't going to do you no harm to keep up your old friendship. One day Master David's going to be master of Greenleaf and Dragonard Hill. He can make you overseer like Master Peter did with your Pa.'

'Ma, stop planning my life.'

'Tim, there's something you ain't telling me.'

Already loping down the path, Tim called, 'Ma, stop imagining things.'

Maybelle watched her son continue down the hill in the sun, suspecting that, yes, definitely, he was trying to hide some deep secret from her. She wondered how long it would take her to find out. Maybelle was more interested in the battles on Greenleaf and Dragonard Hill than the war about which she heard white people whispering – the so-called 'Civil War.'

*   *   *

Maybelle, Ham, and David Abdee ate the midday meal at the scrubbed pine table in the kitchen at Greenleaf; Maybelle never used the dining-room except for entertaining Peter Abdee; David had spent most of his boyhood here and was used to the informality of sitting with Ham and Maybelle as members of one family.

Ham discussed the crops at Greenleaf during the meal of fried chicken, grits, bean salad which Maybelle had prepared; she cut generous pieces of berry pie and drowned them in rich cream as David repeated what few stories he knew about Dragonard Hill.

David spooned the cream from his dish and, glancing at Maybelle's kitchen helper, the brown-skinned girl named Hettie, he confided, 'I'm always the happier here at Greenleaf than home.'

'Maybe you should move back here, Master David,' Ham reached for his tin cup to wash down the dessert with a deep gulp of coffee. He held his pie plate to Maybelle for a second serving and raised his eyes to the ceiling, adding, 'We don't see much of the one gent who lives here.'

David frowned. 'To be honest, Ham, that's why I could never move back here. Because of Alphonse.'

'Change places with him,' Ham suggested. 'You come here and lets him go there.'

'Ham!' Maybelle chided. 'Sometimes I thinks you has goober peas for brains! That's just what Alphonse wants! He'd like nothing better than for Master David to give up his room to him at Dragonard Hill.'

David smiled at Maybelle's outspoken honesty and readiness to defend him. She was the closest thing to a mother he knew; she even surpassed the role of a 'mammy' which many white children enjoyed with black women; David felt no racial differences between Ham, Maybelle and himself; he was pleased that they possessed the civilized comforts of Greenleaf and often wished they could know the true feeling of freedom.

He asked, 'Maybelle, you ever hears of a black man named John Brown?'

Glancing at Hettie loitering behind them. Maybelle answered guardedly, 'I hears lots of talk these days. Talk that don't has nothing to do with me.' She remembered Tim also mentioning that same name – John Brown – to her only a few hours before and wondered if it was more than a coincidence.

David had an idea and, pressing it, he said, 'Now you know my step-sister in Boston, Veronica?'

Maybelle beamed at the mention of the name. 'Miss Veronica? How can I ever forget that dear girl?'

Ham agreed. 'Miss Veronica, she's a mighty special lady to us.'

David's pale face tightened; he said with contempt, 'Lots of people remember Veronica, but mostly for the wrong reason. People remember Veronica because she married a black man.'

'You do speak straight out with it, Master David,' Ham said.

'What else am I to say, Ham? That Veronica married beneath her . . . "social station"?'

Maybelle threw back her head and laughed. 'That's

48

the Abdee in you talking. Just like an Abdee. You and your step-sisters has different mothers so it must be something in your Pa's blood that makes you all so different from other white folks hereabouts.'

'I know little about my Abdee blood,' David confessed. 'In that way I'm like you. Like a black person. I know little about my background. Even my father doesn't know much about his father, my grandfather, Richard Abdee, except that he was the whipmaster on the island of St Kitts. The Dragonard.'

'That's where your pa got the name for the plantation Dragonard Hill. Didn't your grandpa have a place down in The Indies called Dragonard? Named after his job of being the public whipmaster down there?'

'Father never speaks about either of his parents. I know his mother is dead. That he was raised by a black woman and brought here as a slave by mistake. That the Selbys found out he was white and raised him almost like a son. As for his father — ' David shook his head. 'Abdees don't have much to be proud of. And let me tell you this, too. No matter how hard father tries, neighbours will always complain that he's too liberal.'

Pausing, David's blue eyes brightened and he asked, 'Have you ever thought about going north? Leaving Greenleaf?'

Maybelle and Ham looked at one another and then both glanced at Hettie idling by the side door. Their concern escaped David; he proceeded, 'I'm not asking you to say yes or no today. I'm only suggesting you think about it. You could travel with me.'

'Travel with . . . you?' Maybelle's eyes rounded with surprise.

Ham asked, 'You going to visit Miss Veronica and Royal? In Boston?'

'I don't know what I'm going to do. But if this war

49

gets worse and comes closer to us, we'll have to think about doing something.'

Ham leaned forward, whispering, 'But if you go north, Master David, you'd be leaving the plantation to Alphonse. Think about that. And another thing – '

David interrupted, 'I wouldn't be going for good! But you might think about travelling with me.'

He now noticed Hettie lingering behind them, Ham and Maybelle's sudden nervousness, and Maybelle becoming increasingly fidgety over the conversation. He leaned back in his chair, saying, 'We can talk about this later. I'm only formulating a plan. I know Veronica really loves you. I could get papers – '

Maybelle reached for the bone-handled spatula, saying, 'You gets nothing but more berry pie. And if you say you can't eats it then I'll give you a swat. Remember how I use to do?'

Cutting another piece of pie for David, Maybelle called, 'Hettie, quit standing around like some ninny. Bring more hot coffee for us and then start preparing the tray for Master Alphonse. You know how irritable he gets if he don't has his coffee served to him before he shaves himself.'

*   *   *

Alphonse St Cloude still lay in bed when Hettie entered his upstairs room with a tray of coffee and hot cinnamon bread; Alphonse was toying with his phallus beneath the cotton sheet, thinking again about rich white women in New Orleans when he looked up and saw Hettie standing in the open door. He shouted, 'You forget how to knock, wench?'

'I guess I forgets because of whats I just hears downstairs.'

'What are you talking about, nigger bitch?' He was irritated both by the intrusion and her crude attempt to be artful.

'I hears Master David talk about slave-running.'

'Slave-running? David Abdee?'

'Yes. Master David's visiting downstairs right this minute, trying to convince Ham and Maybelle to go north.' Hettie added to keep Alphonse's attention. 'Master David's planning to get a whole lot of niggers to run. I couldn't hear much more because he keep his voice real low.'

'David? Go north?'

'North where he's got a sister. The one who married a big-shot nigger from Dragonard Hill.'

'Veronica.' Alphonse had never met Veronica Abdee but he had certainly heard the stories how she had married a house slave from Dragonard Hill who had educated himself up north and now worked as a banker.

He said, 'Maybe you do have some sense, nigger gal.'

Hettie set down the tray alongside the bed, unable to avoid seeing the bulge under the sheet.

Alphonse had forgotten about New Orleans, though, and was now thinking how he could use this information about David Abdee, envisioning how he could start a campaign against him in the neighbourhood; the local farmers and patrollers had always been suspicious of the Abdee family.

But then Alphonse remembered what the local farmers thought about him, how they hated him, knowing that he was the illegitimate offspring of Peter Abdee and a free woman of colour. If there was one thing which the local white people loathed and mistrusted more than a Negro slave, it was a free Negro.

New Orleans! Yes! That was where he would go! He would start his campaign there where people were cautious of Abolitionists but gave more credence to a free person of colour.

Suddenly, feeling Hettie's hand on his crotch, Alphonse pushed her away and screamed, 'How dare you? How dare you touch me, nigger bitch?'

' "Nigger" ', she glared at him; she knew he had black blood in his veins, too.

'Yes, nigger,' he shouted. 'Only white ladies can touch me.'

Hettie rested one hand on her hip, saying, 'You maybe likes white ladies. But you better get a taste for coloured gals who can helps you be master of Dragonard Hill.'

'Girl, what shit you talking?'

Hettie turned her back to the bed and, peering into the mirror hanging over the mahogany bureau, she airily answered, 'I maybe nigger to you but I ain't dumb as some black gals.'

'Say what you mean!'

'I know how some black gals do anything to get a hold of that pecker of yours. I admits it. I likes what I sees under that sheet. But I ain't going to get down on these knees and beg for it. I going to bargain for it. That's what. Bargain.'

'Bargain? Hell, it's too late for bargains. You already let the cat out of the bag. You already told me about David Abdee wanting to run slaves to the north.'

'You'll want to hear more, though. You'll need me for spying.'

'Maybe.' Alphonse studied Hettie's curvaceous buttocks as she stood curling her hair in the mirror. He added, 'Fact is, gal, you spy for me and I might give you some pecker.'

Facing him she smirked and said, 'I warns you, Master Alphonse. Just a little bit won't do me much good.' She glanced again toward the lump under the sheet and scuffed toward the door, calling, 'Better be danged good, Master Alphonse, because this gal's a power poker.'

' "Power poker"? What's that?'

Reaching toward the door, Hettie said, 'It ain't no card game. Not the kind of poker playing I does.'

She rolled one shoulder at Alphonse, repeating, 'Power poker. You'll see . . . Master, sir.'

Chapter Three

PETIT JOUR

Candles twinkled inside etched crystal globes. Piano music floated through the air redolent with perfume and cigar smoke. Gracious palm fronds drooped over the backs of scarlet velvet love-seats. Tonight was busy as usual at Petit Jour on Rampart Street, the most infamous bordello in the city of New Orleans.

The nightly activity, the gay hubbub, the music, singing and laughter thrilled Condesa Veradaga despite the fact that she had been the madam here for almost two decades. She dipped her white ostrich fan toward planters from Natchez as she moved through the crowded room; she congratulated herself at still keeping her true identity unknown, that she had been born Victoria Abdee – one of the twin daughters sired by Peter Abdee of Dragonard Hill Plantation – but everyone in New Orleans knew her only as a titled lady from Havana.

'Good evening, Condesa Veradaga.'

'Bonsoir, Madame La Comtesse.'

'Countess, honey, you're getting younger every year!'

The Condesa Veradaga – Victoria Abdee, or 'Vicky' as her family had called her – proceeded through a swagged archway connecting two parlours; she held the train of her emerald green satin gown in one hand and acknowledged each call from her guests.

Creole gentlemen. Confederate officers. Rich planters. Prosperous tradesmen. Visitors to New Orleans with enough cash to lavish on the most beautiful prostitutes in New Orleans. Petit Jour attracted the rich and the decadent, the spoiled and depraved, the pampered and seekers of the unusual. What delights the girls at Petit Jour could not supply their visitors in the upstairs bedrooms, they exhibited on the top floor where dramatic entertainments were presented twice nightly in a candle-lit theatre.

Vicky slowed as she passed the chemin de fer table in the second parlour; she noted that a young Creole gentleman was not betting too heavily against the house; she did not want the young man to lose too much money and raise the wrath of the family. The Creoles were the descendants of the original settlers in New Orleans, proud French and Spanish families whose patronage gave Vicky a stamp of approval enjoyed by no other bordello in New Orleans.

Moving from the gambling room, Vicky decided to climb the stairs to the attic theatre and inspect the preparations for tonight's show. She graciously stepped aside as a doddering old white-haired man was being escorted toward the steps by two blonde girls dressed in identical red satin corsets and black webbed stockings.

Old Herman Weller might not be able to keep up his prick, Vicky thought as she watched the buxom girls escort the octogenarian client up the carpeted steps, but he pays well to watch Luella and Suella play with each other in bed and jerk away at his liver-stained old sausage!

Again, reaching to mount the steps, Vicky heard the broad accents of three men seated in chairs grouped round a small table below the banister. She remembered the three strangers arriving a few hours ago; she had been told by a maid that the three men came from Philadelphia, that they were in New Orleans buying cotton for northern mills but everyone in the city was wary of Northern spies.

Vicky paused, eager to catch part of their conversation; the three Yankees had consumed enough champagne to forget about guarding their conversation.

'The pack train never made it to New Orleans.'

'I told you they should have come down the river.'

'The river would have been too obvious,' argued the third man. 'An overland route was the safest way. But two weeks have gone by and the guns still haven't arrived in New Orleans. And nobody's heard a word from Captain Horner. Nothing.' He then leaned forward to proceed with more details.

Vicky, realizing she could no longer eavesdrop, leaned over the carved walnut banister, graciously saying, 'Gentlemen, may I welcome you to Petit Jour? I am Condesa Veradaga.'

'Countess.' The tallest gentleman quickly jumped to his feet. 'We offer you our compliments on your hospitality.'

'You must take full advantage of it,' Vicky said, still flirtatious in her middle years; she looked much younger in the candle-lit parlour than she did in the broad light of day; her red hair was exquisitely dressed with elaborate ringlets and her powdered breasts stood temptingly inside the gown's tightly laced bodice.

'Your establishment was highly recommended, Condesa,' said the second man, now also rising from his Louis Quinze chair.

Vicky noticed that the second man was more drunk than his friends. She asked, 'You gentlemen are northerners, yes?'

The three strangers quickly exchanged glances.

Gathering her crackling skirt, Vicky light-heartedly said, 'May you enjoy southern hospitality, gentlemen. May you even broaden your knowledge of your enemy's little surprises in my theatre upstairs.'

'Oh, we've heard talk about your show, Condesa Veradaga.'

'Hearing is one thing. Seeing is another.' Vicky moved to mount the stairs but stopped when a maid approached her with a small white card.

'Excuse me, gentlemen,' Vicky said and stepped toward a white marble statue of a satyr where the maid could speak privately to her.

The maid, a Negress dressed in a black dress and a crisply starched white apron, said, 'There's a young man wanting to visit here, Countess. He looks white alright, but – '

'You think he might be coloured.' Vicky did not allow coloured men in as clients; she did not want to risk offending her white clientele.

'He is lighter than any coloured man I ever sees. But something about him ain't right.'

'What's his name?'

The maid held the embossed calling card toward Vicky. Vicky read 'Alphonse St Cloude' on the expensively engraved card; the surname was familiar to her; she had long ago sent an octoroon woman by that same name to Dragonard Hill, a young coloured beauty to serve as a governess to her young half-brother, David. Vicky had subsequently heard that Chloe St Cloude though had borne her father a son and lived now at Dragonard Hill as her father's mistress.

Tucking the card down into her powdered cleavage, Vicky asked, 'Where does Monsieur St Cloude say he's from?'

'Up-country, Countess. He says he's a planter.'

'Does he mention the name of his plantation?'

'Greenleaf.'

Greenleaf! Vicky smiled. 'Yes,' she thought. 'Of course. It must be the same man. Alphonse St Cloude.

The illegitimate son of Chloe St Cloude.' She said to the maid, 'Escort Monsieur St Cloude upstairs to the theatre. Tell him the show will begin in a few moments. Then tell Eunice to join me. I have a little job for her to do.'

Eunice, a prostitute from Natchez, affected fine breeding; Vicky employed her because she had seen enough free gentlemen of colour to know what kind of ladies attracted their interest; Eunice enjoyed making love to men with coloured blood and was adept at making them believe they had shattered all social castes by defiling a fine white lady.

*   *   *

Young Negro attendants, dressed in loin-cloths and their sinewy bodies gleaming with oil, snuffed out alternate candles in the theatre's crystal wall sconces, slowly dimming the stage area for tonight's theatrical presentation, 'Gilding the Lily'.

A flaxen-haired white girl slowly emerged from the shadow to stand motionless in front of the guests congregated on chairs and lounging on chaise longues; a tinkle of a harpsichord sounded from off-stage as the girl gracefully raised both arms, exhibiting green gossamer-thin lace stretching from her arms to her legs, a finely worked pattern portraying the foliage of a verdant tropical plant.

Next, two women strolled onto the stage shaking their heads disapprovingly as they studied the naked girl standing with her arms held upstretched as if she were a plant; the two women did not speak, only miming that the girl should be taller, greener, more voluptuous.

One woman lifted a watering can and proceeded to water the girl's bare feet. But the watering can was empty. The two women shrugged and, looking around the stage for water, one woman pointed off-stage; she then beckoned someone to come toward them.

A tall naked Negro slowly ambled onto the stage; the two women pointed to the empty watering can and then at the girl costumed as a plant; the Negro understood; he stepped forward and, pulling back the black foreskin of his outsize penis, he urinated into the watering can as the harpsichord music became more delirious.

The two women, pleased with their resourcefulness, turned to pour the yellow urine on the bare feet of the girl.

The girl writhed, twisting her arms, spinning, twirling, the gossamer-thin lace floating, enlargening as if the plant were growing. Also at this moment, one black man silently ran across the stage holding a large translucent disc, a glass representation of the sun and its rays.

The two women, thrilled with their garden work, warmed by the sun, began pulling off their hats, gloves, blouses, skirts; they beckoned for two more Negroes off-stage.

Vicky sat behind a black scrim which separated her from the stage area; she watched the crowd becoming gradually excited as the two white ladies threw themselves at the subsequent black actors, lunging at their limp phalluses, holding the watering cans for the men to simulate they were urinating into and pouring on them, grasping to take the phalluses into their hands, mouths, any orifice.

Waiting until the white girl – the plant – was being mounted by the sun, Vicky turned to the ladylike prostitute, Eunice, sitting alongside her. She said, 'Go, sit alongside Monsieur St Cloude.'

'He is handsome, Countess,' Eunice said, adjusting her heirloom pearls. 'Is he rich?'

59

'I'll tell you more about him later. Just remember you're a lady, a fine lady of breeding. Now go and report to me later.'

Vicky, sitting alone, ignoring the orgy developing on the stage area, scanned the excited onlookers for the three Yankees, the three men who had talked about a pack train of guns, about soldiers disappearing in the wilderness.

Victoria Abdee, the Condesa Veradaga and proprietress of Petit Jour, was not a patriotic creature; the three Yankees ultimately did not represent a political threat to her, rather a harbinger of changes for prostitution in New Orleans.

*   *   *

Vicky sipped strong black coffee in her office on the ground floor of Petit Jour after the second show and counted the evening's profits.

A knock disturbed her and, calling for the person to enter, Vicky raised her eyes to see the prostitute, Eunice, looking dishevelled, tired and dressed now in a crumpled robe.

Eunice closed the door behind her, saying, 'That Monsieur St Cloude is quite a talker.'

Gauging Eunice's spent appearance, Vicky grunted, 'It looks like he's pretty good at a few other things.'

Eunice sank into a chair, saying, 'I have seen big cocks, Countess, but nothing like that one.'

Vicky was not interested in his sexual endowments; she asked, 'What did he talk about?'

'Himself and other ladies. He kept talking about black girls who wanted to pester him. But how he only likes white ladies . . .'

Vicky had heard such stories before; she had known

other light-skinned free men of colour who shunned –
blatantly avoided – sexual contact with Negroes. She
asked, 'Did he speak more about his plantation?'

'Yes,' Eunice answered, rubbing her tired legs. 'He's
come to town to get financing for expansion. He plans
to take over a neighbouring plantation. A nest of Abolitionists.'

'Abolitionists?'

'Monsieur St Cloude also talked quite a bit about his
family. Trying to impress me, the same old thing. He
called them "nigger lovers", says he has a half-brother
who's sickly. A fellow who does nothing but read
books about human rights.'

'Half-brother?'

Eunice pulled at her hair now hanging in greasy
shanks, saying, 'Mr Alphonse called his half-brother
David. He mocked him as "Master David". And, if you
ask me, Countess – '

'David? An Abolitionist?'

Eunice detected the recognition in Vicky's voice. She
asked, 'You know him? This David?'

Ignoring the question, Vicky reached toward the
night's earnings and rose from her chair. 'You did good,
Eunice. You take this gold. Keep quiet about Monsieur
St Cloude for the moment. Now go to the stable and
send me Paulie.'

Minutes later, Vicky Abdee sat with the small Negro
named Paulie, a man diminutive as a jockey; she gave
him instructions how to ride north-west from New
Orleans, to find a town called Troy, then a plantation
named Dragonard Hill. She told him to search out the
cook named Posey at the main house of Dragonard Hill,
not to say who had sent him, only to tell Posey that
Alphonse St Cloude had come to New Orleans and was
spreading rumours that David Abdee was an Abolitionist.

Vicky did not know if there was any truth to Alphonse's story, but, if there was, the only person at Dragonard who could stop David's stupid plan was the invincible Posey. Victoria Abdee had little faith in – nor love for – her family, but she did not want to see any more spilling of their blood.

Chapter Four

POLITICS

Maybelle sat in the parlour of Greenleaf with a cup of afternoon tea, taking a brief respite from her kitchen chores, lovingly appraising the parlour's rose-patterned carpet, the chintz-covered chairs, the damask curtains, china figurines, all possessions which she had come to cherish as her own. Basking in comfort, Maybelle planned how she would roast a chicken for her husband's supper tonight before they retired to their upstairs bedroom in solitude now that Alphonse St Cloude had gone south to New Orleans.

Maybelle treasured the days at Greenleaf when Alphonse went to New Orleans; she was relieved not to have to wait on him hand and foot, to tolerate his arrogant and often ridiculous demands; but, most enjoyable of all, Maybelle and Ham could indulge themselves in the comforts of Greenleaf as a married couple.

Anticipating the liberty of making love to Ham tonight without being mindful of disturbing Alphonse down the hallway, Maybelle closed her eyes and took a deep sigh. She and Ham had been married now for more than thirty years and their love-making was still as lusty, passionate and inventive as any younger couple.

Ham, potent and vigorous, satisfied Maybelle best when she was free to cry out, to vent her passion as he knelt between her thighs, cradling her against his groin, driving deeply inside her. Maybelle sat now in the parlour, envisaging the love they would enjoy tonight, knowing that she would first spoil him, not only by preparing his favourite supper and mixing him a whisky toddy, but also to linger in the foreplay he enjoyed so much, to allow him to salivate noisily as he worked his tongue into her vagina, to be free to moan and thrash her arms against the mattress as he chewed on her sexual lips.

Maybelle became so absorbed in these thoughts about love-making that she did not see the carriage from Dragonard Hill until it stopped in the driveway outside the parlour's bow-fronted windows.

Hearing voices, she sprang to her feet and pulled back the curtains. She saw Master Peter alighting from the carriage, holding his hand to Chloe St Cloude, who was followed by . . . Posey!

Posey? What's he doing here? Maybelle wondered as she quickly composed herself. She could not remember the last time that Posey had visited Greenleaf.

Maybelle watched Peter Abdee bid Chloe goodbye and turn toward the stables. She guessed he was probably going to visit Ham. Next, she saw Chloe moved toward the front door but – not surprising to Maybelle – Posey gathered his skirts and walked stiffly around the side of the house to the back door.

Maybelle graciously greeted Chloe at the front door, extending both arms, saying, 'Miss Chloe, mam! It's been too long since I've seen you!'

Chloe returned the warm greeting but was unable to hide an edginess which confused Maybelle. She folded her shawl and removed her bonnet, saying, 'I came to collect a few things from my room.' Moving toward the stairway, she hesitated, 'Alphonse has gone to New Orleans, yes?'

'He left last Tuesday.' Maybelle held Chloe's bonnet and wrap.

Chloe continued upstairs, saying with forced concern, 'And you're fine? And Ham?'

'We're both fine, thank you, Miss Chloe, mam.' Maybelle stood at the bottom of the stairs, realizing that Chloe did not want to be followed, that she wanted to rummage alone through the rooms which had once been her governess quarters at the top of the house.

A voice asked sharply from beneath the staircase, 'What's the matter? Don't you keep coffee around here?'

Maybelle saw Posey standing in the doorway which led to the kitchen.

'Miss Posey!' Maybelle always used the title 'Miss' when addressing the male cook from Dragonard Hill. 'I didn't see you sneak in the back door!'

'I sneak no place, woman,' Posey sniffed. 'But I knows my place, I don't use no front door.'

Maybelle had always suspected that Posey harboured jealousy over the freedom which she and Ham enjoyed here at Greenleaf; she rushed forward, saying, 'I wish I had your knack of running a kitchen, Miss Posey. There'll be coffee for you and Miss Chloe in a jiffy.'

'You need a good kitchen girl.'

'I got Hettie. But she ain't nothing to brag about.'

'Take a wooden spoon to her! That always works! A good strong wooden spoon. Give the wench a few hard smacks on her bottom with that and you'll get some results!'

Minutes later, Maybelle and Posey sat across the scrubbed pine table from one another; three coffee cups set in front of them, but, so far, Chloe had still not come downstairs to join them.

Maybelle strained to make conversation with Miss Posey; she could easily forget that Posey was a man dressed as a woman; her difficulty in talking to him was his stiff, demanding veneer. And Posey seemed even more imperious, almost hostile today; he questioned Maybelle like a government inspector.

He asked, 'You buy much groceries from the general store in Carterville?'

'No. We eat from the garden and orchard.'

'You cooks better than those niggers in slave shacks? Better than possum and turnip greens?'

'Ham hasn't complained,' Maybelle answered, nervous now even to offer Posey a piece of her raisin cake. She was certain that he would find it dry, hard, inferior to anything which emerged from the kitchen of Dragonard Hill.

'You cook special dishes for him?'

'Him?' Maybelle then realised who Posey meant. 'Alphonse! Oh, he always complains. But he never talks bad about the cooking he eats from your kitchen, Miss Posey.'

'That's because he never eats none,' Posey snapped, ruffling his apron, adding, 'Least, none that I know of.'

'Not even when he comes to visit his mother?'

'Miss Chloe, she's a good woman. She keeps her no-good son out of my way.'

'But, Master Alphonse —'

'Alphonse! He's no "Master"! He's just plain nigger Alphonse!'

'But he's Master Peter's son, Miss Posey,' Maybelle said in a hushed voice. 'We must never forget that.'

Ignoring Maybelle's remark, Posey held his head high, demanding, 'Tell me why Alphonse has gone to New Orleans.'

'Miss Posey! You be remarkable! How you know all what's happening? Alphonse lives here at Greenleaf and you know he's gone to New Orleans!'

66

'I got ears' Posey said, determined not to divulge that he had had a secret visitor from New Orleans yesterday, a black man who had come to the kitchen annex posing as a pedlar but, in reality, had been a messenger with dreadful stories about Alphonse spreading lies in New Orleans about Master David Abdee.

Maybelle said, 'Now if there's anybody who should go to New Orleans to visit, it's Master David. He's been talking about travelling. But talking about going north.'

'North?' Posey's voice became instantly attentive. 'Master David going north?'

'To Boston.'

'Why Boston?'

'Miss Posey, you knows Master David's half-sister lives there. You also knows how dear Miss Veronica is.'

'But Miss Veronica —' Posey stopped and looked at Maybelle. 'Master David, he say anything else about his visit?'

'What do you mean?'

'Like maybe he wants to take a . . . few people with him?'

The question stunned Maybelle; she gaped at Posey, wondering how he had learned that David had asked her and Ham to accompany him on a trip to the north. Or was Posey just fishing for details?

'Don't play act with me, woman,' Posey ordered. 'You're as black as me and us blacks have to trust one another. Least us house blacks. Now tell me, what else Master David says when he comes here. Does he talk like he has feelings like Miss Veronica?'

'Feelings?'

'What white folks call politics.'

'Why you asking me these questions, Miss Posey?

Why you come to my kitchen after all these years and start –'

Posey sat to the edge of his chair, saying, 'Listen, and listen to me good, woman. People are mighty suspicious these days. There's a big war being fought if you knows it or nots. It has to do with some niggers. It also has to do with greed. Now, you and me both know Alphonse is greedy. He'd do anything to get Master Peter to name him as his rightful heir. Even go so far as to spread stories in New Orleans that Master David is planning to run slaves to . . . Boston.'

'Alphonse doing that?' Maybelle gasped. 'Alphonse St Cloude is spreading those stories in New Orleans about Master David?'

Posey sat back in his chair, asking, 'How I knows what's Alphonse be doing in that town? I be sitting here in your kitchen!'

'Posey, this is no time to play games. You said yourself us niggers must stick together.'

'Don't put words in my mouth, woman. You just ask yourself where Alphonse heard such stories?'

'You don't believe them?'

'I don't believe nothing except that Alphonse is a greedy snake and if Master David does have any radical plans, then –' Posey shook his head, saying, 'You just better do some house-cleaning, woman. House-cleaning for . . . spies.'

They both heard Chloe's footsteps on the stairs; Posey puckered his lips, shook his head and held his finger threateningly at Maybelle to keep her mouth shut about the facts he had just divulged; his role also included being protector to Miss Chloe, who, in the last few days had been acting strange, quiet, secretly tormented. Posey did not want Chloe to hear them gossiping about her son.

*   *   *

Maybelle carefully weighed Posey's questions and warnings long after Peter Abdee had collected Chloe St Cloude and Posey from the kitchen and returned to Dragonard Hill. Maybelle became increasingly puzzled how Posey could lead such an isolated life in the Louisiana wilderness yet know about stories which Alphonse was supposedly spreading in New Orleans.

Determined to enjoy this time alone in the house, Maybelle prepared Ham a fine supper that evening and, as an extra surprise, she served it by candlelight in the dining-room with delicate china dishes and thin crystal goblets, which she filled not with wine but cold milk from the springhouse.

Ham joked about the dining-room's finery, comparing it to the days when they lived in a long-legged hut in the slave quarters of Dragonard Hill.

He said, 'We has Miss Veronica to thank for all this. She was the one to put the notion in her daddy's head for us to live here like white folks after Matty Kate died and there was nobody left to take care of this house.'

'Miss Veronica, she's our guardian angel all right,' Maybelle agreed, rising from the table to gather their plates; she and Ham never mentioned their brief glimpse of Veronica's involvement in the Abolitionist movement and she did not want to discuss it now.

'Gal, you seem down tonight.'

Maybelle lingered alongside the table, thinking about Veronica, David and Miss Posey's story as she stared at the candles flickering in the baroque silver candlesticks, the small flames gleaming in the highly polished mahogany table-top.

'Honey, you look like you going to cry!' Ham said, reaching to pat his wife's chocolate smooth forearm.

Maybelle did not reply; she thought about this house, their easy life here and remembered the hardships they had known in the slave-quarters.

Ham, seeing his wife's face sadden as she stood staring into the candles, rose from the chair to comfort her sudden melancholy.

Maybelle instantly responded to his warmth; she sank her head against Ham's broad shoulder and wailed, 'Oh, honey man, what if we lose all this?'

'Lose it? What for you talk like this, Maybelle? Talk about losing?'

Miss Posey's warnings swirled around inside Maybelle's brain; she hated herself for sounding weak but she continued, 'The war! The greed! People fighting for this! Fighting for that!'

Putting his hand under her chin, Ham said, 'Honey, white people starts this war. We niggers don't have much say in it. But folks claims that if the North wins it, then more black folks can live like you and me. To live like people. Not like farm animals locked in some hut. The war is being fought to free us black folks from slavery. You tell me you wants to enjoy china plates and eggshell thin glasses but lets no other black gal has the same privileges you do?'

Tears welled in Maybelle's eyes as she begged, 'Oh, Ham! Don't make me feel ashamed of myself!'

'I'm just telling you what that war's all about, honey. What those northern states are talking. What their Mr Lincoln, president man, is saying about the white folks down here. We lucky, you and me. We be Master Peter's pets. And Master Peter he's more lenient than most white slave-owners. Also young Master David, he be a good white man, too. But just thinks if some devil like Master

Alphonse was ever to gets control of this place! Just think about that! Then we have to fights a war, too!'

Maybelle snuggled closer against Ham's warm body, saying, 'I don't want to think about nothing, honey man. I just wants to be together with you.'

Ham lowered one hand to Maybelle's breasts and gently began working one nipple; he also nibbled at her ear, whispering, 'Your man protects you, baby.'

Maybelle, cupping Ham's hand with her own, remembered his words about not being selfish; she thought how right he was, that she must be willing to sacrifice for other black people to enjoy the same physical comforts she enjoyed here at Greenleaf and how easily she could lose everything if Alphonse seized control of the plantation.

Ham leaned forward and, brushing her cheek with a tender kiss, he murmured, 'We must look to our blessings while we has them, baby.'

Maybelle nodded, feeling a strong surge of love inside her breast for Ham; she whispered, 'Take me upstairs, baby.'

Ham wrapped one arm around his wife's shoulder and led her from the dining-room in silence; he held her tightly against him as they slowly progressed up the stairs, down the hallway and into their bedroom; Maybelle's earlier intentions to spoil Ham suddenly were abandoned as he now became more dominant with her.

Undressing Maybelle, Ham softly reassured her that only their love was important and everlasting; he pulled back Maybelle's treasured linen sheets and, crawling naked into bed alongside her, he pressed against her warm body; he turned his words into kisses, exploring her mouth with his tongue, inching his phallus toward her feminine mound, beginning to punctuate his kisses with long, steady, deepening thrusts of his phallus, actions to reassure Maybelle of their spiritual union as husband and wife, their most important possession at Greenleaf, in the whole world.

*   *   *

Chloe St Cloude lay that same night curled alongside Peter Abdee in their bedroom at Dragonard Hill; neither Chloe nor Peter spoke to one another; Chloe's hand rested on his bare shoulder, her long black hair, unpinned from its chignon, spread across the white pillows; Peter's arm cradled Chloe against his chest, he held one long leg sideways on the mattress for Chloe's small body to enjoy a harbour close to his nakedness.

Peter had noticed Chloe's change of attitude since Alphonse had last visited her here at Dragonard Hill; Chloe had become even more silent and introspective after Alphonse had gone to New Orleans; she had hardly said a word since their visit to Greenleaf this afternoon. But Peter respected her privacy and did not press her for an explanation of this unusual mood.

Nor did Chloe want to burden Peter with her latest problems; she had long ago abandoned hope that she and Peter could legally claim their son, perhaps someday recognize Alphonse as the offspring of their love. Chloe knew that Peter had suffered many disappointments in his life; she did not want to draw attention to Alphonse's latest avarice.

Nevertheless, Chloe could not put Alphonse's new crime from her mind; she had suspected that he might do something heinous and this afternoon she had gone to Greenleaf to substantiate her suspicions.

Chloe had discovered this afternoon that Alphonse had stolen the small pewter jewel cask from her former living-quarters at Greenleaf, that he had taken the jewellery she had left there, the keepsakes she had owned before coming to Dragonard Hill, valuables she kept at Greenleaf because they did not belong in her life with Peter Abdee — bracelets, brooches, rings, necklaces which had belonged to her aunt.

It was not the loss of the valuables which troubled Chloe as much as the knowledge that her own flesh and blood would steal from her. And, consequently, Chloe realized that if she was a dutiful mother she must follow Alphonse to New Orleans and confront him about his unscrupulous ways; she feared that a young man who would steal from his own mother would stop at nothing.

Chloe lay silently in bed, thinking how she must keep Peter from being suspicious about her sudden trip to New Orleans, to keep him from suspecting, too, that she suffered guilt about bearing a child out of wedlock, not providing her son with a proper father, and now swearing to herself — as a mother — to do whatever she could do to save Alphonse from complete moral ruin. She saw it as her maternal duty.

*   *   *

David Abdee sat alone in darkness down the wide hallway from his father and Chloe's bedroom; he looked over the driveway climbing the hill from the public road which ran between the small towns of Carterville and Troy, a travellers' artery which represented access to the outside world to David Abdee; the road strangely frightened him.

Loneliness had always pervaded David's life; his only memory of companionable happiness rested in his childhood at Greenleaf; he had played there with Tim and had enjoyed Ham and Maybelle as parents; he knew

73

he could never regain those lost days, nor did David envision himself ever taking a sweetheart, marrying some young lady and siring his own family: when David Abdee searched within himself for sexual desires, he found nothing, physical attraction to no-one.

Sitting in the darkness of his bedroom and staring blankly down at the public road, David resigned himself to the fact that he must begin accompanying his father on trips to Carterville and Troy, to become part of the neighbouring community despite his distaste for the people, to seize these days and move about the countryside with no fears of accidentally running into Alphonse St Cloude.

David pledged to himself tonight that he must try to be more sociable, to go into the world where men talked about crops, politics, slaves and . . . war.

Closing his eyes, David wondered why he did not have a stronger character. He considered the rest of his family. Veronica had followed her own instincts; she had done the unthinkable, had married a black man and moved away to the North. And what about Vicky? David barely remembered his scandalous half-sister who had married a crippled Cuban aristocrat. No-one ever heard from Vicky any more but, if she was still alive she was probably still following her own convictions too. And then there had been Imogen, another strong individual, even if her strength had led to her death.

'So why don't you give yourself a chance?' David asked himself. 'Why don't you see if you can find a place for yourself in the world? You must try to put all your efforts into your own ambitions. You must decide what *you* want to do.'

'But what do you want to do?' David asked himself. 'Go north? Leave Dragonard Hill? Stop being a recluse? Perhaps even prove your hidden beliefs that black people like Maybelle and Ham must not be slaves? Try to help some of the people who have been good to you?'

David felt a gnawing, nervous pain in the pit of his stomach; he cursed his weakness, knowing that if he were to be strong, he must accept the fact that a war was being fought, join like every other self-respecting man, both in the North and the South.

*　　*　　*

The same night. An owl hooting in the stillness of towering pine trees. Bats making silent dives against the indigo sky. Roots curling like snakes over the mossy forest bed. And Tim sitting forlornly on a fallen log in the one small patch of land which joined Greenleaf to Dragonard Hill, a gulch in the pine forest which lay to the north of Witcherly Plantation, the land separating the bulk of Peter Abdee's two properties.

It was here, in the pine gulch common to both Greenleaf and Dragonard Hill that Tim had buried the guns and ammunition, a spot known only to him.

Tim had returned here tonight in the moonlight and was considering his parents urging him to get married rather than worrying about what he would do with the guns, nor nervously brooding again about his five friends telling other slaves about ambushing the pack train. He felt a constant driving in his loins for women, true, and often satisfied his desires with slave wenches. But he did not want to sire a child who would be born into slavery.

By the same token though, Tim hated a life of promiscuity, of constantly finding new wenches to satisfy his lusts, to compare his conquests with Bullshot, Sebbie, the other young Negroes who held him in esteem. Many girls sought out Tim for a lover; the latest girl to be chasing him was Hettie, his mother's kitchen helper.

Tim knew that his mother would be angry if she learned he had ever made love to Hettie; he knew his mother disapproved of the girl, thinking he could do better.

Also Tim agreed with his mother; he would never take a girl like Hettie for a wife.

'But who is there?' he asked himself as he sat on the log in the moonlight, poking at clumps of moss with a stick. 'What choice do I have? Who am I? Nothing more than a . . . slave.'

Despite his rejection of Hettie as a possible wife, Tim thought of her body, her fulsome breasts, her teasing glances and he felt his penis harden inside his tow trousers.

No, Tim did not want to masturbate. He did not want to spill his seed on the ground.

Rising from the log, Tim began walking, trying to change his train of thoughts, to ease the blood making the crown of his phallus stand large and strong against the rough weave of his trousers.

Then Tim thought again about the guns buried beneath the ground; they were valuable, true, but also they were dangerous and could condemn him to death. But how else could a slave gain his freedom? Wait for the Northerners to ride to all the plantations like saviours?

Tim broke the stick and, tossing it to the ground, he walked swiftly through the brush toward the slave-quarters. He would try to forget his problems, to eradicate his lust, in a night of much-needed sleep free of dreams about murdering soldiers and the consequences of possessing illegal guns.

*　　*　　*

Bullshot, not knowing where Tim had gone on this night when the moon shone large and silver in the sky, had seen the kitchen girl, Hettie, loitering between the woodshed and the springhouse. Hettie had at first refused to divulge why she was out so late, so far away from her kitchen pallet in the main house, but, soon, she confessed that she also was looking for Tim.

'What you wants Tim for, gal?' Bullshot was younger than Tim but equally endowed sexually to satisfy Hettie; she had not repelled his advances and they now stood naked together inside the small woodshed, their clothes piled on the chopping block.

Hettie, having refused to lie on the floor and get wood chips stuck to her bare skin, leaned against one wall as Bullshot stood between her stretched legs. She wrapped her arms around his strong neck and, letting him hoist her higher onto his hard phallus, she whispered, 'Why you talks about Tim when you making pudding with me?'

'Just wants to know,' Bullshot answered, holding Hettie by her buttocks to guide her slim body up and down on him in slow, easy, satisfying movements. 'Just wants to knows if you be a gal looking for pecker or if you wants to lift your skirt for Tim being his Pa's overseer.'

'Could be,' Hettie twisted herself in Bullshot's strong grip, making his phallus sink deeper, stir farther inside her.

'You ain't liking this?'

'I like lots of things.'

'What's you likes, gal?'

'I likes this.'

'What else? What else you likes? Tell me.'

'I likes . . .' Hettie threw back her head and considered the question.

Bullshot, quickening his rhythm like a terrier, asked, 'You likes sucking?'

'Maybe.'

'You likes serving lunch?'

' "Serving lunch"?'

'Letting me eats your pudding pie.'

'Uh-huh, I likes that.'

'What else?'

'I likes men who be . . . powerful.'

'Likes me? Likes this?' He drove deeper, harder.

Hettie, tilting her head, her mind distant from Bullshot's eagerness to please her, answered, 'I gets tired being slop girl. I wants to run a big house, too. I wants to . . .'

Bullshot was beginning to feel an increasing sensation, a thrill spread to his groin which told him he was about to ejaculate his seed. His strokes quickened; his breathing became stronger; he slapped one broad hand on Hettie's buttocks and bit his lower lip as he moved her up and down faster on his phallus.

'Nigger!' she squealed, suddenly struggling. 'Lets me go!'

'Shssh, gal.'

'Nigger, you stop!'

'Enjoy, gal. Lets yourself enjoy.'

'Enjoy?' she repeated, beginning to push hard at Bullshot's chest. 'Enjoy having your sucker planted in my belly? I no fool, man.'

Hettie freed herself from Bullshot's grip; he had crested so close to his orgasm, though, that he was not going to allow her to flee; he pushed her down to her knees, ordering, 'Open your mouth, gal. Open your mouth and don't talk. Just suck. Just suck that pecker and –'

Kneeling, Hettie obeyed Bullshot because he was a

78

strong man and would surely rape her if she did not follow his orders. But as she felt his seed fill her mouth, cascade down her throat, she thought about Tim, about Master Alphonse, about taking the seed of any man who was powerful enough to assist her in her ambitions to rise in the slave hierarchy of Greenleaf Plantation, or, with luck, Dragonard Hill.

*　　　*　　　*

Sebbie, nineteen-years-old and more daring than either Bullshot or Tim in the pursuit of his love-making, sneaked away from the slave-quarters on Greenleaf that same night and ran along the shadowy public road to a small cabin owned by white people.

Sebbie's first meeting with the white woman had been in the small town of Troy, glances which signalled to youthful Sebbie that the older but firm-bodied white woman desired him; she subsequently spoke a few hurried words to him as she sat alone in a parked wagon, nervous conversation which told Sebbie that she was willing to break local taboos and make love to a black male; she finally whispered an invitation to Sebbie to meet her at the cabin she shared with her husband – and when her husband would be away in Carterville on business. The white woman did not disclose the nature of her husband's business; she did not even tell Sebbie her name, only that she was called Loraine.

Sebbie stood tonight by a cluster of cottonwoods, looking at the small cabin, no lights flickering inside the windows. He remembered Loraine's large green eyes, her fair skin, hair which was red as strawberries; he also recalled Loraine's nervousness and this excited him because he suspected that it cloaked unfulfilled passions, that she must be frustrated in making love to her husband and would be unselfish to a man who could satisfy her.

A whisper disturbed the stillness of the night; Sebbie looked behind him and saw a figure standing in nearby trees; he immediately recognized the curvaceous shape and his heart began to beat both with excitement and terror. He knew what happened to black men who were discovered making love to a white woman. He fleetingly wondered if this was a trap.

But a strong sexual urge made Sebbie cross the small patch of dirt separating him from the trees where Loraine stood waiting for him; he approached her, beginning to ask, 'You be alone –'

'Don't worry. My husband, he's gone for the night. Nobody's here except me.'

She reached for his hand and, stroking his smoothly skinned arm, she murmured, 'You are so young.'

Sebbie did not know how to reply; the hardness forming inside his trousers betrayed that he was very much a mature male.

Stepping closer, Sebbie put a hand on her slim shoulder and then began to finger her long silky red hair.

Enjoying his fascination with her, Loraine closed her eyes and rubbed her head against his attentive hand like a cat, whispering, 'I seen you in Troy for so long. But I never thought we'd be together.'

The frank statement encouraged Sebbie; he stepped even closer, now pushing his firmness against her midsection; he did not know if she would be offended if he kissed her; he did not know what deportment white women expected from young black men.

The touch of Sebbie's persistent long fingers against her made Loraine smile. She opened her eyes; she held Sebbie's stare as, slowly, she reached for his groin; she said, 'You are like some angel sent to me tonight.'

The words pleased Sebbie; he nodded, saying, 'I be whatever you wants me to be. Angel. Visiting man. A good friend.'

'You promise?'

He nodded, realizing she was very lonely.

'You won't tell nobody about us? No matter what we do?'

He shook his head.

'You will do . . . everything with me?'

'Everything.'

'And I can do everything to you?'

'Whatever you wishes, Miss Loraine, Mam.'

'No. Don't call me by my name. Don't call me nothing. We just be two people. We just be me and you.'

Dropping to her knees in front of him, Loraine pressed her cheek against the bulge in Sebbie's trousers, whispering 'My angel. My brown angel who finally comes to visit me.'

Sebbie unknotted the rope from his trousers and, as the roughly woven garb fell to the ground, his penis bobbed large and hard in front of Loraine's face.

She knelt staring at the penis, leaning forward to kiss its crown, to suck it, to smooth her tongue along one side, to cup Sebbie's testicles in the palm of her hand as she gently rubbed the black penis back and forth against her white face.

Sebie fell to his knees alongside her and, feeling her breasts through the thin cotton dress, he whispered, 'Are we safe here? Nobody's about, you sure?'

Loraine did not answer the question; she held his eyes as he kept working her breasts, saying, 'You are so young . . . so beautiful . . . so shiny like brown satin.'

'I be a nigger, Mam.'

' "Nigger",' she repeated. 'A beautiful . . . black man. For me. Just for me. Just you and me.'

She flung her arms around Sebbie; her desperate kisses and clinging arms assured him that she did not know true physical love; he reached under the skirt of her dress and, feeling the moisture between her legs, he knew she was ready, eager to take him.

Soon, Sebbie lay naked alongside Loraine, her white legs scissored around his slim black thighs as he drove into her thrusting thighs; she held his long tongue in her mouth as he toyed with her nipples, twisting herself more hungrily on him as he drove deeper, more quickly inside her.

Pulling back her head in the moonlight, Loraine closed her eyes as Sebbie again fingered her hair; he slowed his sexual strokes into her whilst he pet the long strawberry-coloured tresses falling over her naked shoulders.

She whispered, 'You likes what you see?'

'Hmmm.'

'And what do you see?'

'I see us making love.'

'Making love. A black man. And a white . . . lady.'

'You be a beautiful lady.'

She smiled. 'Do you want to do this again?'

'Tonight?'

'Tonight and every night we can.'

'We won't get caught?'

'We will be very careful, won't we? We will be very, very careful and make love as much as we can, as hard as we can, as deep and true as we can.'

Flinging her thin white arms around his chest, she whispered, 'Come deeper inside me. Come deeper. I can't get enough of you. You are so big but I want more. I want you again. I want more of you again and again and again.'

Sebbie quickly worked to satisfy her, receiving satisfaction himself by watching this strange white woman losing herself with him – nothing but an Abdee slave from Greenleaf Plantation.

Chapter Five

OCTOROON DANDY

The Confederacy repelled the Northern troops at Bull Run and Mannasas in the summer of 1861; spirits ran high in New Orleans for General Beauregard's victories and that city's famous battalion, the Washington Artillery, which had fought bravely to defeat the Yankee troops in the initial battles between the Northern and Southern states.

The war caused no immediate concern in New Orleans; Forts Jackson and St Phillip guarded the Mississippi River; the citizens believed that the fighting – raging far away now in Missouri – was too distant, too far removed from their homes to endanger them.

Alphonse St Cloude found an air of excitement, even frivolity in New Orleans. Young men gaily formed militiae to join General Beauregard but the majority of the New Orleans citizenry was too cosmopolitan, too entrenched in European ways, to feel a true part of any continental American dispute.

Contaminated by the decadent glamour of New Orleans, Alphonse soon forgot his original intention for coming to the city to sow seeds of Abolitionist propaganda about David Abdee and win support for himself to gain control someday soon of Dragonard Hill.

Alphonse visited the absinthe houses and gaming parlours of the French Quarter; he idled with dandies, enjoying foreign wines in the bar of the St Charles Hotel; he visited his tailor on Dumaine Street and made nightly assignations at Petit Jour on Rampart Street with the white prostitute, Eunice, a woman whom he still believed to be a high-born lady who used the bordello as he did himself – a place for sexual assignations.

Money became Alphonse's main concern; he had received less payment than he had anticipated for two filigree golden brooches and an emerald bracelet he had stolen from his mother. He quickly squandered that money and next pawned a necklace set with opals and diamonds, plus three jade rings and now was left with a few golden chains, three sapphire rings and a strand of pearls clasped with diamonds.

But, true to his proud nature, Alphonse did not confide in Eunice about his precarious financial position. Instead, he affected more extravagant habits at their meetings, still believing her to be rich and totally infatuated with him; he was waiting for her to announce imminently that she was ready to leave her husband, to run away with him with all the valuables she could glean from her own household.

Eunice – following Vicky's strict orders – did not openly claim but she strongly implied that she was both born of, and married into, an old Creole family; Alphonse knew that gentlemen were meant to respect such privacies and he politely refrained from pressing for details.

The facts of his own background also remained vague. But Eunice openly referred to the gens de couleur libre living in New Orleans, extolling these free coloured peoples accumulating wealth and living in great style. Alphonse interpreted these remarks as Eunice's knowledge, or suspicion, that he had a drop or two of coloured blood in his veins but that she did not care, that his fine looks, his wealth, his stylish manners, obliterated any discrimination she might feel against a non-white.

Eunice went even further in her praise of the gens de couleur libre in New Orleans. She confessed, 'I often envy the octoroon mistresses of rich planters who live across Esplanade Ridge. They seem so snug, so serene in their pretty little cottages waiting for their lovers to come from those up-river plantations.' Eunice sat along-side Alphonse on a settee in a small upstairs parlour at Petit Jour; she toyed with the ruffles on his lawn shirt as she spoke.

Alphonse kissed her hand and then leant forward to refill her champagne glass; he replied, 'Men often are more jealous lovers than women. Especially if they are paying the bills.'

Running one finger down his neck, Eunice said, 'Yes, I have heard terrible stories of violence. How you planters even lock your mistresses in shackles. But you would not be violent. You are far too much of a gentleman, monsieur.'

'Gentleman?' He shrugged, saying, 'I can only conduct myself how I was raised.'

Eunice leant forward and, kissing his ear, she said, 'But you are different from other gentlemen. There is something of the . . . animal in you, monsieur.'

Alphonse felt himself harden; Eunice had again managed to arouse him before they had even fallen onto the bed. He asked, 'You find me different than other men in your life?'

The question surprisingly sobered her mood; she reached for her fluted champagne glass and pouted, 'I do not ask you about your life, monsieur. Please do not ask about mine.'

'You are not happy!' he blurted out. 'Confess it! But who is? We at least have passion!'

86

' "Passion"? Passion is not everything, monsieur! There is decorum. Protocol. Many other things. Now all I hear is war, these battles, our boring victories over General McDowell!'

Alphonse had frequently wondered if Eunice was married to a Creole aristocrat, a gentleman who had already gone off to fight with General Beauregard. He asked instead, 'Would you be upset if I joined one of the new militia?'

Eunice dropped her head, the candlelight catching the jet beads glistening in her glossy black hair; she said, 'I must confess, monsieur, I have been waiting for you to say that. You are a land-owner and must obviously be concerned about your vast holdings.'

Alphonse seized the moment to elaborate on his fanciful story. 'I also have a family who would be glad if I went to war! If I got killed by some Yankee! My family is weak. They would probably free all the niggers while I was fighting to protect what good people believe in! That is the only reason I come here to New Orleans. To make legal preparations for my plantation in the event I should get killed.'

'Your brother, he is that crazy, to give all your land to the black people?'

Putting his hand on Eunice's knee, Alphonse smiled, saying, 'You do not talk about yourself, dear lady. I will not talk about myself.'

Eunice toyed with the emerald necklace spread over her milk-white throat; she answered, 'Yes, we have talked too much already. When you gave me this little trinket I saw you were upset.' She reached down her breast and lifted the pearl necklace which Alphonse had given her tonight on his arrival.

Little trinket! Alphonse had wanted to sell the pearls and pay his landlady; he realized they did not compare in value to the emeralds she wore. But it had been no measly gift, no 'little trinket'.

Eunice raised his hand to her breasts, saying, 'Do you think I'm bold, monsieur? Do you think I am brazen to want us to make love? To forget about wars and families?'

Alphonse set down his own glass, answering, 'Your boldness is what excites me, even makes me think that you and I —' He stopped; he shook his head, saying, 'You make me talk too much.'

Pulling her toward him, Alphonse tasted the sweetness of her mouth and felt his phallus increase in strength as he thought about himself making love to a white woman, a fine lady who treated him like a white person himself.

Alphonse lowered his mouth to Eunice's throat, resting one hand on her breast, pressing the gown's richness to work an excitement; he listened to her gasping, waiting until she leaned back her head on the settee and closed her eyes before he lifted her in his arms.

Carrying Eunice toward the bed, Alphonse continued kissing her, fighting an urge to be overtly dominant with her, still not knowing what liberties her gentility would permit him to indulge.

Soon, after they both undressed themselves, Eunice lay demurely under the linen counterpane and Alphonse stood naked on the carpet alongside the bed; he threw back the covering and, staring at Eunice's white skin, he held his phallus in one hand, enjoying its feeling with a slowly moving fist, bending forward to kiss the dark mound between Eunice's thighs.

Eunice tossed her head back and forth on the pillows, gasping as Alphonse began darting his tongue into her feminine cleft; he soon raised both hands to her thighs to stretch a wider path for his oral enjoyment; then, hearing Eunice beginning to beg him to make love to her, he moved his tongue up her body, licking a wild pattern over her abdomen, her sides, around both breasts, and firmly encircling one nipple – then, the other – with his tightly pressing lips; he nibbled at each rosy bud with his teeth and, listening to Eunice gasping louder, he moved quickly onto her convulsing body.

Flinging her arms around him, Eunice pleaded, 'You hurt me . . . You bit me . . . You tease me so much . . . Oh, Alphonse . . .'

'Do I hurt you too much?'

'I don't know . . . I don't know . . .'

'Do you want to know?'

'I don't know what I want . . . I want so much from you . . . Oh, Alphonse, you are so rough with me sometimes . . . Alphonse, I feel so . . . abandoned.'

The words, the whining reproaches, the uncertainty in Eunice's voice drove Alphonse into a further frenzy; he no longer could resist from ramming the blunt crown of his phallus between her legs; he positioned his hands on the mattress to pump against her hungry, reaching, clinging body.

Despite the rapidity of his slick strokes, Alphonse still could not stop thinking as he made love to Eunice, could not keep from wondering if she indeed was an heiress or wife of some rich Creole gentleman, a white woman who not only desired him but could also finance his ambitions. He had to find out more about this mysterious Eunice.

*   *   *

Vicky examined the necklace of matched pearls which Alphonse had given to Eunice a few hours earlier and listened to the prostitute's report about how she suspected Alphonse was faring in New Orleans. Eunice said, 'He does not seem to be lacking for money. He is always finely dressed.'

'Clothes mean nothing!' Vicky studied the pearls, saying, 'Dandies are born with a knack for conning tailors out of clothes! But jewellers – ah, they are a different breed of tradesmen. They do not so easily part with their goods. And these pearls, they are old. Alphonse St Cloude could have bought them, but I doubt that. He also could have stolen them. That is more likely.'

Dropping the rope of pearls into the drawer of her pearwood desk, Vicky said, 'Keep bleeding him for money.'

'You have a special interest in him, Condesa.'

'Yes, I do,' Vicky said but did not want to divulge her reason. She rose from her chair behind the desk and said, 'There is another matter I'd like to talk about, Eunice.'

'Yes, Condesa.'

'Your special interest in Catherine.' Vicky stood in front of Eunice's chair, arching one thin eyebrow as she stared down at the sudden terror flashing in Eunice's eyes.

Vicky folded both hands behind her back and proceeded to pace the office. She said, 'You know I forbid my girls to develop romantic attachments between one another. But because you have been doing such a good job with Alphonse St Cloude, I have not mentioned your nightly visits to Catherine's bed.'

Eunice remained sitting motionless on the chair.

'Don't be nervous. I'm not going to punish you. Nor am I going to send one of you away. I'm just letting you know that I'm no fool.'

'Thank you, Condesa.' The words were barely louder than a whisper.

'Just be discreet,' Vicky said, walking toward her. 'And continue satisfying Alphonse St Cloude. Find out exactly why he is in New Orleans. Where he gets these jewels. Which reminds me –'

Vicky held out her hands towards Eunice, 'The other necklace, my dear.'

Eunice's hands flew to her throat; she had forgotten the jewels which Vicky loaned her to wear at tonight's assignation with Alphonse to impress upon him that she was a rich Creole gentlewoman.

Vicky took the precious necklace, and telling Eunice to go to her room and get some sleep, she waited until the prostitute left before she looked down at the jewels.

The emeralds had been a gift from her husband, Conde Juan Carlos Veradaga upon their son's first birthday. Juan Carlos had given Vicky precious gifts on each and every birthday, christening, anniversary, feastday of little Juanito.

Thinking about her son, Vicky wondered what Juanito looked like now. He was a grown man. Had his father died as she had heard from a traveller? Had little Juanito inherited a title along with the family's plantation – the finca – and sugar mill in Cuba?

Stuffing the emeralds into a leather pouch, Vicky put the thoughts of Juanito out of her mind. She was strong at forgetting things but it was becoming difficult lately to forget about her son. Why was that? Because she was getting older?

'Stop it', she told herself. 'If you must think of the past, if you want to think about families, then think what you are going to do for your father, for poor, sickly David, for Dragonard Hill.'

Vicky recalled the words which her messenger had brought back from Posey, that David Abdee was a recluse and certainly not notorious in the neighbourhood as an Abolitionist. She smiled, though, at the rumour which her messenger had brought back from the small town of Troy; she had instructed him to ask specifically about 'Victoria Abdee' at the general store there and, true to her suspicions, she was still remembered as the neighbourhood's most licentious white female. She wondered what the backwoods patrollers would say if they sampled some of the pleasures she offered at Petit Jour.

* * *

Eunice, spent from simulating sexual excitement for Alphonse St Cloude and repeating the stories she had carefully rehearsed with Vicky about the background of a well-born Creole lady, fell into a deep sleep as soon as she collapsed onto her bed. Dawn was lighting the sky beyond the pulled draperies and Eunice did not want to awaken until noon.

Feeling the gentle touch of warm skin against her nakedness, Eunice stretched her arms to welcome a familiar body alongside her in the snug bed. She knew without opening her eyes that it was Catherine.

'Was he dreadful again?' Catherine whispered, curling around Eunice's naked body. 'That awful Alphonse St Cloude?'

'Don't,' Eunice groaned, pulling Catherine's arm around her. 'Don't mention him or any other man to me.'

'You should have seen the horror I got stuck with tonight. If there's anything worse than a big prick, then it's a little one, a little, tiny, red prick like a rooster that goes poke, poke, poke . . .'

Catherine gently jabbed Eunice's back to illustrate her meaning of a small, erect penis jabbing into her vagina.

Shrugging her shoulder for Catherine to desist, Eunice pleaded, 'Don't, my darling. I'm tired. Exhausted.'

'How long will it last, this cat and mouse game she has you playing?'

Eunice did not answer.

'You can't keep playing this grand lady part forever. Somebody will surely tell him sooner or later you're nothing but a hooker.'

Still Eunice did not reply.

Catherine began kissing Eunice's back, murmuring, 'I'm sorry, my love. I know you are tired. It's just that we get so little time together. So few moments. And when I think of that arrogant Alphonse fancy-pants making love to you, probably even thinking he can marry you, I get so jealous I could scratch his eyes out.'

'She knows.'

A silence followed Eunice's sudden announcement.

'She knows all about us.'

Catherine sat upright in bed.

'There's nothing to be alarmed about,' Eunice drowsily assured her lover in the darkness of the heavily draped room. 'As long as I keep Alphonse on the string, you and I are safe.'

'Are you certain?'

'Very certain. Our ace in the hole is Alphonse St Cloude. Funny, isn't it? A man keeping us together. Now be a good girl and go to sleep.'

Eunice pulled flaxen-haired Catherine back down to the mattress and, snuggling closer to her, she drifted back to sleep.

Catherine waited until she heard Eunice breathing heavily in her sleep before she slipped down the mattress, between Eunice's naked legs, crouched under the covers to tongue Eunice's vagina whilst masturbating herself. She also was tired but moments such as these

93

were the only times lately for her to satisfy the genuine love she felt for Eunice.

Tasting Eunice's womanhood, Catherine thought of phalluses and how men normally assumed the aggressive position on a female, on her lover.

Eunice always cleansed herself after making love with a client but, as Catherine tasted her personal sweetness, she thought that Alphonse St Cloude's phallus only a few hours ago had penetrated this same channel.

Remembering the small penis of the last man who had mounted her this evening, Catherine tongued more deeply into Eunice and thought about Alphonse's large proportions which Eunice had jokingly described to her.

Catherine curled her finger between her own thighs, working, grasping, struggling to rush her orgasm so she, too, could fall asleep. She knew she would have a restless night if she did not consummate some form of love with Eunice; a nightly mating had come to be her only way of reassuring herself that she could love someone, to eradicate the guilt of her profession.

But the image of phalluses remained in her mind, bloodhard organs which defiled women, throbbing crowns which worked only to pleasure themselves, cascading sperm which made the proud phallus diminish in size, obliterating a man's passion for a woman.

'Only a woman knows what another woman's passions are,' Catherine told herself as she felt her mouth fill with the taste of Eunice's vagina; she longed to hold her lover's breasts in both hands, to knead them as she rubbed her knee between Eunice's thigh to create a warm fulfilling friction for her womanhood.

Catherine often wished that Eunice was awake for their late night love matings. But at other times she excited herself by thinking that she was sexually seducing Eunice without her knowledge, that Eunice

was a woman who disapproved of such practices between females and Catherine could only seize these
liberties when Eunice was asleep.

It was with this fantasy, that she had waited for
Eunice to fall asleep before pursuing this forbidden
love, that Catherine finally felt excitement tingle inside
her; she fought not to hear Eunice's heavy breathing in
her weary sleep, imagining instead that Eunice was
gasping with excitement, that soon she would be tasting
her rich love liquid, that Eunice was awakening from
her sleep and, realizing that Catherine was performing
the most personal act on her, allowed herself to revel
in the union.

Catherine finally gasped with these thoughts propel-
ling her excitement, an imaginary scene which had to
suffice between lovers until the time might arrive when
they did not have to submit themselves to men, that
she did not even have to fantasize that this act was
surreptitious, a day when they could make love like
other people in the world.

Chapter Six

THE BROUGHAM

Chloe St Cloude rode in comfort from Dragonard Hill in Peter Abdee's brougham, a black carriage pulled by a white horse, through sleepy country towns and over furrowed roads which led south to New Orleans. Finally, after a long, arduous day's travel, the mud-splattered carriage reached the bayou road crowded with mule-drawn carts and plodding teams of oxen, all headed for New Orleans.

Peter Abdee had insisted that the Dragonard Hill coachman, Bernard, drive Chloe to New Orleans when she announced she must settle her aunt's estate; Peter did not want Chloe to take a public coach and had even insisted she travel with trustworthy slaves for protection against highway-men or patrollers. Chloe argued that she needed no escort but accepted Peter's insistence on the brougham, fearing that she might arouse his suspicions about the true purpose of her mission to New Orleans.

The traffic grew thicker as the Dragonard Hill brougham moved slowly down St Charles Avenue; Chloe noticed many uniformed men clattering past her on horseback; this was her first realization that a war was truly being fought in the south; the confrontation between the northern and the southern states was more of an actuality here in New Orleans than in up-country towns and plantations isolated from current affairs.

Determined to find some clue of Alphonse's where-

96

abouts, Chloe ignored the troops passing on horseback, the cannons rumbling alongside the wide thoroughfare on large wooden wheels, the tented supply wagons streaming toward Lake Pontchartrain. Chloe concentrated instead on where she would make her first inquiry about Alphonse; she leant forward in the buttoned leather seat, calling to the coachman, 'Bernard, take me to Rampart Street. I do not remember the exact address. But I'll recognize the house when I see it.'

Bernard called over his shoulder, 'Don't you wants to go to your aunt's house, Miss Chloe? The journey's been long and dusty. You must be plum tuckered out, mam.'

Chloe could not even confide in Bernard that the story about her aunt was a canard, a fib she had concocted about the old lady, Tante Marie, who had groomed her from childhood to be a lady and presented her to society at the Octoroon Ball on Orleans Street; Tante Marie had long ago died and left little more in her estate except the pewter casket of jewels and a small cottage beyond Esplanade Ridge where she herself had once been subsidized as a mistress by an up-country gentleman.

The cottage might not even be standing, Chloe knew, but she would worry about that later. She answered, 'No, Bernard. Take me first to Rampart Street.' She then quickly added for conviction, 'I must get the keys!'

Bernard snapped the whip over the horses' heads and turned down Baronne Street, entering a jungle of ornate iron balconies and tall narrow buildings lining the wooden sidewalks of the French Quarter. Chloe sat rigidly in the back of the brougham, racking her brains for the exact location of the house to which she had been summoned years ago, the bordello called Petit Jour, where a titled lady had first engaged her to be a governess to a frail young boy named David Abdee. Chloe had never divulged to Peter Abdee that it was the Condesa Veradaga – his daughter, Vicky – who had arranged for her to go to Greenleaf Plantation.

*　　*　　*

Vicky lay in bed at this late evening hour, enjoying the last few moments of privacy before she had to greet her male guests in the parlour. She sipped a cup of mint tea, considering how she must soon change the theme of the theatricals upstairs; she was pleased with the response for her tableau, 'Gilding the Lily' and wondered what the next theatrical should be.

Men are excited by seeing women make love to one another, Vicky told herself. They also enjoy watching other men making love to a woman, even occasionally watching the act of sodomy between two men.

'But sodomy is often so filthy. Physically unclean. Shitty. The secret is to keep everything attractive,' she thought as she lay propped on a bank of paisley covered pillows. 'But I suspect that men also are secretly intrigued by enemas. What the French call "la douche". Perhaps I could devise some way of using enemas, a douche, on the stage. Would that be too outrageous? Would I be treading where angels –'

Vicky's thoughts of hygiene and staged sodomy were interrupted by a knock on the bedroom door; she called for the person to enter and a black maid came in, announcing, 'Condesa, Madame St Cloude wishes to see you.'

'Madame St Cloude?' Vicky at first thought the announcement was a joke, that Eunice had come to report playfully that Alphonse had proposed marriage to her.

She said, 'Show the bitch in.'

The maid exited and, a few moments later, Vicky

stared in amazement at a small woman approaching the foot of her bed, a finely-boned creature dressed in a bonnet, a long coat with a cape to the waist, gloves and a reticule, handsomely cut clothes but completely covered with dust.

'Condesa Veradaga,' the small woman said, standing nervously before her. 'Excuse me for disturbing you, my name is Chloe St Cloude. Perhaps you do not remember me, but –'

'Of course I remember you!' Vicky answered from the bed, appraising the travel-weary woman. 'This is a surprise. I have not seen you in – how long has it been since I placed that advertisement in the newspaper?'

'Many years have passed, Condesa, since I went to Greenleaf as a governess for your half-brother.'

'You wear your age well,' Vicky complimented, waving for Chloe to sit on a tufted silk chair near the bed.

'The Condesa looks beautiful as before,' Chloe complimented, sitting on the edge of the chair to avoid spoiling it with dust.

Vicky asked, 'How is my father?'

'He is well, Condesa.'

'But he does not send his regards to me.' It was not a question.

'He does not know I've come here. To this house. He knows nothing about you nor the black woman, Naomi, who used to be mistress here.'

'Naomi?' Vicky shrugged, confessing, 'She's probably dead by now. I have not heard from Naomi in years, since she went to Havana. But let us not talk about Petit Jour. Tell me about you, Chloe. You haven't run away from my father, have you?'

'No, Condesa. Your father is kind to me. More than kind. But –'

Vicky held her eyes on the small, genteel woman. She secretly admired the grace which Chloe St Cloude had retained.

'This is difficult to say, Condesa.' Chloe proceeded, 'Your father and I have been close friends. Even . . . lovers. We have a son. His name is Alphonse. I know that he has come to New Orleans. I also realize that you meet many young men . . .'

Vicky never divulged everything she knew. She asked, 'Why do you worry about your son?'

'I am afraid that Alphonse might cause trouble.'

'Trouble? For whom? Is he a troublesome young man?'

'He is arrogant, ambitious and –' Chloe shook her head.

Vicky no longer could keep up the charade. She propped more pillows behind herself, nonchalantly adding, 'Avaricious. Selfish. Vain. Spoiled. And devilishly handsome. I would add all those words to the list which describes Alphonse St Cloude.'

'Then he has been here?'

Vicky nodded. 'Alphonse St Cloude comes here almost every night of the week.'

'You are certain?'

'Behind you, on the table, there are some pearls. Perhaps you recognize them?'

Chloe turned in the chair to look at the pearls but stopped. She murmured, 'Why should I doubt you? If you say Alphonse comes here then it must be him.'

'Let me tell you this. I do not know why you want to see him. But I think your son will only cause you misery. Forget about him. Sons grow up into men. Think about yourself. Your own life.'

'But Alphonse is part of me. My flesh and blood,' Chloe wailed, then added more softly, 'Oh, if he were not so defiant!'

'Defiant? Ah, I understand defiance. I know to what lengths "defiant" people will go. No mother – nor father – can stop a defiant child. I know! I speak as one!'

'But Alphonse stole from me! Stole from his own mother to come to New Orleans! But why does he waste his time here? What does he want in this city? What is so important that he would steal pearls, a few diamonds, gold rings from his mother?'

Vicky was not surprised to hear Chloe confess that the pearls belonged to her. She expanded on the theory she had developed about Alphonse, saying, 'Your son is determined to inherit Dragonard Hill, that's why he behaves like he does.'

'How can he do that by coming to New Orleans?'

'By spreading rumours.'

'About whom?'

'David. My father. Perhaps even you.'

'But rumours about what?' Chloe shook her head in confusion.

'Slavery is the issue of the day. The reasons behind this war.'

'But Alphonse is not a slave. My son was born a free man.'

Vicky realized that Chloe was innocent, a woman still protected from the world's cruelty. She began, 'Alphonse is coloured. He is eliminated from his inheritance by being both illegitimate and coloured. That is why he is spreading stories about Abolitionists and slave runners.'

'Abolitionists?' Chloe gasped, 'Whom does he accuse?'

'David.'

'That is a lie. David seldom leaves his room. Nobody would believe Alphonse.'

'Come, come. You have been living with my father

long enough to know that Dragonard Hill is unlike any other plantation. My father allows his slaves many liberties abhorrent to his neighbours. You have probably also heard stories about my sister, Veronica.'

Fixing her eyes on the small octoroon woman, Vicky explained, 'No, Chloe, it would not be difficult to convince people that Dragonard Hill harbours Abolitionists.'

'But what would Alphonse gain by that? And why does he come to New Orleans to spread stories?'

A pounding on the door disturbed them and a maid rushed into the room with the news about Chloe's coachman, Bernard, being attacked on the street and that an angry crowd was gathering around the front courtyard.

*   *   *

Alphonse St Cloude had awakened that same day late in the afternoon, feeling a strange presentiment of trouble; he quickly dispelled his anxiety, convincing himself that he was merely worried about money, that no handsome young man had ever starved to death on the streets of New Orleans.

He shaved himself and chose his clothes with great care; he was meeting Eunice again tonight on Rampart Street and he had decided to ask her to marry him; the question would force Eunice to say if she was married or not to a rich Creole.

Reinforced by his decision to be aggressive, Alphonse emerged from the rooms he rented on Chartres Street and decided to walk down to the levee; he bought four oysters on the half shell from a vendor and strolled through the early evening crowd gathered in Place d'Armes; he jingled the few coins in his pockets and decided to go early to Petit Jour, to try his luck at gambling before Eunice arrived for their assignation.

Alphone immediately recognized the dusty black brougham waiting on Rampart Street in front of Petit Jour; he first thought that Peter Abdee had come to New Orleans, that he was inside the bordello. Of course! What other establishment would he visit? Alphonse also was certain that David Abdee would never be brave enough to visit such a notorious place. Never! David was too cowardly even to come to the city!

Smiling when he recognized the Negro coachman, Bernard, dozing above the brougham's white horse, Alphonse told himself, 'See, I knew this evening would bring me good luck! Look what's fallen into my lap! Better than if I had even planned it!'

Alphonse threw a stone at Bernard to awaken him, then loudly jeered for passersby to hear, 'Come to town to run more slaves, Bernard? Well, you won't find them there! Not in a whorehouse! Or did Master David get the hiding places mixed up this time? Did Veronica Abdee tell her brother the wrong house to find runaway niggers?"

Bernard, although still half-asleep, recognized Alphonse St Cloude. But he could not understand why he was shouting at him, why the crowd was collecting on both sides of the street, why people were beginning to look angrily at him.

'You have some nerve in war-time, you niggers,' Alphonse taunted; he turned to a group of young soldiers gathering alongside him and explained, 'That's Bernard. A nigger from Dragonard Hill. You know. A spot on the underground railroad. The family that runs slaves to the north.'

Alphonse stood back as the soldiers crowded to drag Bernard from the brougham; he elaborated on his story to the crowd gathering to watch the arrest; he failed to see the four women rush to the iron grille enclosing the courtyard across the street from him.

Vicky's angry shouts at the mob first attracted Alphonse's attention to the courtyard. But the mob swelled around the brougham, pushing Vicky back into the courtyard.

Condesa Veradaga! Alphonse stared at her but quickly stepped out of view when he saw his mother rush to grip Vicky's arm and pull her away from the mob.

'Maman! What is she doing there? It's not Peter Abdee at all! But, Maman!'

He next thought, 'Did she come because of the jewel cask I took? Did she follow me?'

Alphonse's mind then suddenly went blank when he saw other women from Petit Jour gather around Condesa Veradaga, prostitutes still dressed in their kimonos or blankets wrapped around their corsets; he at first did not believe his eyes, but, yes, he clearly saw that one of them was Eunice! She wore only a cotton wrapper and held her arm protectively around a flaxen-haired prostitute; they clung together like lovers.

'The bitch!' he angrily thought. 'She duped me! They've all duped me!'

Word quickly passed along Rampart Street that a black slave-runner had been trapped, that Confederate soldiers were taking him to the Orleans parish jail. But, by this time, Alphonse St Cloude had already disappeared into the crowd.

Chapter Seven

FATHER, SON, SLAVE

David Abdee could not avoid noticing his father wandering aimlessly around Dragonard Hill after Chloe had gone to New Orleans; Peter Abdee seldom spoke at supper and, when he did, his eyes were melancholy; he only became alert when he heard a sound outside the house, glancing to see if Chloe was at last returning home. The first days passed, then one week, then the second week, Chloe still did not come back to Dragonard Hill; no letter nor telegram arrived from her in New Orleans; Bernard did not return with the brougham.

Realizing for the first time how much his father loved Chloe and depended on her both for companionship and energy to perform day-to-day chores, David decided that he must at least try to help lighten his father's slipping spirits; Peter Abdee was beginning to look like an old man; his cornflower blue eyes lost their lustre; he took little pride in his appearance.

David remembered the pledge he had made to himself about participating more in community life and, seeing his father's mood worsen into a depression, he finally suggested that they make a trip together in the buggy to the nearby small town of Troy. Any diversion would serve as medicine.

The late summer afternoon was hot; the sun had burned the low surrounding hills to a crisp brown; Peter held the reins of the sprightly mare and, as the buggy bounced along the dusty country road, David made idle conversation about the ripe crops, the cabin being built beyond Greenleaf Plantation by a new family in the neighbourhood, the expansions on the saw-mill on the outskirts of Troy.

'War's always a time for prosperity,' Peter said, slowing the horse as they approached the plank-fronted buildings lining the dirt road which served as the main street of Troy, Louisiana.

'The place looks lazy as usual.' David saw a yellow dog sprawled on the dirt in front of a cabin; a bleached sign reading 'Inverness Tavern' at a slant from the next doorway, two grimy-faced urchins tugging at a hog to which they had tied a rickety wagon; David smiled at town life in Troy; he did not feel as depressed as he had expected; although conversation with his father had been sparse the outing was obviously beneficial for both of them.

Peter drove the buggy farther down the dusty main street, approaching the empty shack which had once been The Firefly Tea Room. He slowed the horse, gazing down the road at a cloud of dust; the thunder of hooves disappeared in the distance. Peter observed, 'Sounds like we just missed the week's local excitement. Soldiers just rode through Troy.'

'Not patrollers?' David asked.

'No,' Peter shook his head and lifted the reins. 'The weather's too hot for patrollers to be out on horseback. Those can only be soldiers passing through town.'

'Do you really think so?' David surprised himself at being excited by the idea of soldiers in the vicinity. He did not feel frightened nor threatened; he was even curious to learn about the war's progress.

'Hey, nigger lovers!'

Peter and David both looked toward the general store from where the derisive shout had suddenly come.

A second voice sneered, 'You out to free a few more slaves, Abdee?'

Peter appraised the group of patrollers slouched on the porch; local farmers and white labourers who alternated patrolling the public roads for runaway slaves and philanthropic white people who aided them.

David whispered, 'Do you think we should really stay here, Father?'

A third man called from the porch, 'Why ain't that kid there of yours off fighting the war, Abdee?'

Peter replied, 'I don't see you dressed in uniform, Mr Saunders.'

'And I ain't never seen you fighting to save our respect. So don't give us none of your high mucky muck sass, Abdee.'

David urged, 'Father, I think we should go.'

But Peter Abdee ignored David's plea. He called to another man on the porch. 'Bill Cramer, maybe you can tell me what's troubling you and your friends today.'

'The war, that's partly what's riling us.'

Peter responded, 'I'm older than all of you, but I'd probably be the first to go to fight. I've always fought to protect what's mine.'

'That's the trouble with you Abdees,' Cramer answered. 'You think about yourself and shit on the rest of us.'

'If something's bothering you men, come out and say it.'

Dick Dawson stood up and, taking a straw from his mouth, snarled, 'We're wondering if you're going to start freeing your slaves, Abdee.'

'I do what's my business.' Peter showed no signs of being intimidated; his blue eyes suddenly became bright; his words had bite to them.

'What anybody does around here is everybody's business,' announced Billy Cramer. 'One bunch of niggers hears another gaggle of niggers gets freed then they wants free, too.'

'What precisely are you talking about, Mr Cramer?'

'Niggers and freedom, that's what! Niggers running north!'

Peter had always felt a strong loathing for Cramer. He replied, 'I don't think any of my people are about to leave Dragonard Hill nor Greenleaf.'

'Your daughter left you!'

Peter worked his jaw, angrily gripping the buggy whip. 'One daughter moved to Boston. Yes, and another was killed. I'm sure all you gentlemen remember that criminal incident.'

Silence momentarily greeted Peter Abdee's crisp statement, the patrollers on the front porch of the general store glanced at one another.

'What about your son there?' Chuck Saunders asked. 'How does he feel about the war? About some high-minded white folks freeing their slaves?'

Peter began, 'I told you . . .'

But David, standing up alongside his father in the buggy, interrupted, 'You men have obviously been listening to propaganda. But that's the oldest trick in the world. An enemy always tries to get their opponents to fight amongst themselves.'

Laughter followed David's brief speech. But he did not feel embarrassed or disheartened; he felt a fighting spirit for the first time in his life.

Saunders jeered, 'Don't try any of your fancy book-learning on us, young Abdee. We just warning you and your Pappy not to start playing with fire.'

'Fire!' David shouted. 'We start no fires. Not in any metaphorical way you mean.'

'Meta-what?' laughed Cramer.

'Speak English so's we can understand you,' called Benson.

David began to reply but Peter put his hand on David's arm, advising, 'Don't waste your breath.'

Cramer rose from the steps and, tucking his hands into the belt buckled under his protruding stomach, called, 'You Abdees better watch your step or you'll find yourselves protecting that fancy place of yours on the hill like Fort Sumter.'

'We fought off a siege before, and we'll fight one again,' Peter called, snapping the whip over the mare's head.

The wooden spokes on the buggy revolved like pinwheels as Peter and David Abdee drove away from the general store, leaving Troy in the opposite direction to that which the soldiers had ridden.

* * *

Peter Abdee decided to stop at Greenleaf Plantation to warn Ham and Maybelle about the ill feelings in the neighbourhood about the Abdee family, Dragonard Hill and perhaps even themselves.

David, shaken by the confrontation with the patrollers only after he and his father had left Troy, wondered what had given him the courage to speak out so bravely against the surly men. Before today, he had even been too frightened to look any of the louts in the eye.

Maybelle greeted Peter and David from alongside the water pump which was set behind the yellow-roofed house. She called, 'Miss Chloe come home yet from New Orleans, Master Peter?'

Peter, too distracted now to be maudlin about Chloe, answered, 'Business is obviously taking longer than she expected. Where's Ham, Maybelle? I want to talk to both of you.'

'There's trouble,' Maybelle, said, looking from Peter to David and back to Peter again. 'I've never seen such a pair of stormy faces like you two.'

'It's those – ' Peter hopped down from the buggy, ' – God-damned patrollers again.'

Maybelle, seldom hearing Peter use the Lord's name in vain, glanced back to David, then lifted the pail of water she had just filled at the pump. She said, 'Come inside, Master Peter. I'm just fixing to make fresh lemonade. Ham'll be here soon. You two come in the house out of this sun.'

'Where's Tim?' David asked.

'Tim?' Maybelle stared blankly at David. He had not asked Tim's whereabouts in years. She answered, 'Tim's working, I reckon, Master David. Working with a chopping crew down at the fir patch beyond the meadow.'

David turned to his father, saying, 'You go inside with Ham and Maybelle, Father. I won't be long.'

The rich, cool scent of the forest brought childhood memories rushing back to David; he followed a dirt path down the slope from the out-buildings, winding through the pine trees. He remembered how he had played here as a child with Tim, how they had relived stories which Ham had told them about pioneers travelling out to the far western territories, how they had crept through these very same trees, expecting Indians with tomahawks to jump out on them from the branches.

The recollection of childhood bravery, plus his recent confrontation in Troy with the patrollers, made David realize more than ever what an isolated world he had buried himself in, how he was virtually a hermit.

He considered, 'It is a change to be outside the house. To smell fresh air. Hearing a stream tinkle in the distance.' He felt vibrant, alive for the first time in a very long time.

David slowed on the path when he heard the sound of chopping; he knew he was reaching the meadow where the chopping crew was working. He suddenly wondered if he was doing the correct thing, following the right impulse to search out Tim after so many years; they had spoken, yes, but David had never made an effort to see him, nor Tim to see him.

Before David had time to change his mind, he saw three black men approaching him through the lush ferns which drooped over fallen logs. He immediately recognized the tallest Negro as Tim.

'Master David,' Tim blurted, spotting David. 'What brings you here?'

'I don't mean to disturb you,' David instantly realized how foolish his words must sound as soon as he had spoken them, a white man apologizing to one of his father's slaves.

But David could not force himself to speak – nor think – in any different way.

The two other Negroes, Sebbie and Bullshot, immediately slunk back from Tim, only nodding sheepishly at David, murmuring a curt greeting, then hurrying away through the forest.

David was left alone with Tim; he knew he now had to make conversation despite how stupid or stilted his words might seem. 'You working hard today, Tim?'

Tim, as nervous as David, answered, 'That's a drawback of having your pa as overseer. He works you extra hard.'

An awkward silence then fell between the men who had been inseparable boyhood friends; David looked overhead at the towering trees; Tim glanced to see where Sebbie and Bullshot had disappeared; they avoided one another's eyes.

'Your Pa fine?' Tim finally asked.

'He's up at the house. Talking to your Mom and Dad. We ran into a little trouble.'

'Trouble?'

'In Troy,' David shrugged. 'The patrollers there. They decided it was time to warn us. To make a few facts clear to us.'

'Warn you? Patrollers warn . . . Abdees?'

David warmed at Tim's response. Tim had always respected the Abdees. But this respect shamed David. Deference paid to the Abdees – the richest family in the neighbourhood – was due to their large number of slaves.

He asked, 'Tim, can I speak honestly to you?'

Tim shrugged. 'You do what's you want . . . Master David.'

'From what I just heard now in Troy, people think we're slave-runners.'

Tim kicked a clump of dirt with his bare foot, muttering, 'That's stupid.'

'I don't know why people think that,' David continued. 'Maybe somebody just decided to spread rumours.'

'You know who'd that be.'

'Who?'

Tim did not raise his eyes from the ground when he said, 'Alphonse.'

David paused. He answered, 'Alphonse? Could be you're right.'

'I shouldn't speak out like this. My Ma and Pa, they'd both beat me. But – '

'No, I'm sure you're right. Alphonse *would* start such a rumour.'

'Only thing, Alphonse has gone to New Orleans,' Tim said, then raised his head to ask, 'Miss Chloe back yet?'

David shook his head. 'No and my father really misses her. I never knew before how close they are.'

'They be mighty close. Your Pa and Miss Chloe.'

'You have somebody, Tim?'

'Me? A gal friend?'

David nodded.

Tim shook his head, saying, 'No. Nobody in particular. What about you?'

'Me?' David laughed, then, deciding to be brave for the second time today, he said, 'Tim, I don't know how to put this. But I don't quite understand . . . I don't really know if . . .'

Tim blurted out, 'You wants a gal but you don't know how to go about getting one, is that it?'

David's pale cheeks blushed bright red; he confessed, 'Yes and no.'

'You wants me to find a gal?'

'Would you?'

Tim grinned at David, saying, 'You like that?'

David mumbled, 'I guess.'

'Give me a little time then. Not much time. Just enough time to find you a real nice wench . . .'

'Hey! Not just for me, Tim! But you, too.'

Tim looked quickly away from David, suddenly feeling awkward himself. He began, 'Things change. It ain't right to do things like we used to.'

'I certainly don't want you to do anything you don't want to,' David quickly said. 'But I thought maybe we could – '

Tim, wrapping his arm around David's shoulder, said, 'How about tonight?'

'Tonight's fine.' David beamed, feeling like a teenage boy.

'You name the place.'

David pondered the proposal, then said, 'What about that gulch behind Witcherly? The one place where Greenleaf joins Dragonard Hill.'

Tim suddenly eyed David.

'What's the matter? Did I say something wrong?' David remembered that they had played in the gulch as boys.

'No. The gulch be fine,' Tim answered. 'Be there after sundown.'

*　　*　　*

Tim initially thought of procuring Hettie to pleasure himself and David Abdee but, not wanting to arouse his mother's suspicions, he next remembered the tawny-skinned girl, Shira, whom his black friends had bragged was adept at squatting on a man's penis; Tim arranged for Shira to walk with him to the pine gulch which joined Greenleaf to Dragonard Hill, not telling her that another man would be joining them. Shira was eager to make love to Tim, pleasing him first with her mouth and then crouching over his recumbent body with the squatting agility which had won her recognition amongst promiscuous male slaves. Tim did not know exactly at what moment David arrived in the gulch, nor how long he stood in the moonlight watching them; he continued making love to Shira until he realized David stood along-side him. Shira did not show surprise; she reached for David's erect phallus; she worked her contracting vagina to satisfy Tim and leaned to mouth David's penis into further hardness. Tim waited for David to begin driving his penis into Shira's mouth before he pulled away from her and motioned for David to lie on the ground; he watched Shira squatting up and down on David as she now mouthed his phallus; he remembered boyhood days when he and David had shared wenches; he felt young again, relaxed, and knew enjoyment for the first time since he had wrapped the tarpaulins around the muskets and ammunition which lay buried under the exact spot David and Shira used for their love-making. Tim continued to watch David's lean body spread on the mossy bed and hoped this good deed for his childhood friend would ultimately help him to have peace in his dreams about murdering the soldiers.

These thoughts were interrupted when Tim felt Shira pull on his hand; she tugged him toward her, whispering, 'Let me sit on both of your peckers.'

The suggestion surprised Tim; he looked at David for his reaction to Shira's boldness.

Shira whispered, 'You kneels down behind me, Tim. I keep Master David's pecker in me. You drive in alongside him.'

David did not speak but Tim saw that he had shut his eyes, that he was not arguing with Shira's request.

Already leaning forward over David's chest, Shira now motioned where she wanted Tim to kneel behind her, grasping in the darkness to grab a hold on his penis.

The prospect of entering Shira in such a bizarre way excited Tim and, after only a few moments' hesitation, he knelt behind her to jut his large manhood into her vagina now moist and prepared to accommodate both him and David.

Tim felt no extreme sensation at first but, as he strengthened his drives to sink farther into Shira, he felt a closeness to David's penis which made the vagina snug, throbbing, more pleasurable.

Beginning to quicken his rhythm, Tim held his hands on Shira's naked waist as she steadied herself on the ground with both hands. Tim sensed both increasing wetness and a warmth he had never before known, and soon he began to feel even the pulsating of David's penis squeezed closely against his; he tried to dispel the image of a black penis and a white one working alongside each other; he concentrated on his own pleasure until, suddenly, he felt a hand gently grip his scrotum, fingers eager to hold the large sac hanging from the roots of his pumping phallus.

Tim, seeing that Shira still used both hands to steady herself in a squatting position, realized that it was David holding his testicles. He quickly pulled himself from the union but was careful not to allow David to know that the action had repelled him. Tim had closed his eyes all his life to David's physical – and often, emotional – attraction to him. He did not want to encourage such a desire, to add unfulfilled love to David's already burdened conscience. Tim promised himself to help David achieve sexual fulfilment in the one way he knew how, to provide him with wenches despite the lack of emotional fulfilment from such meetings. As much as Tim wanted David to know true happiness, though, he could not provide him with anything else, could not give himself to David, or – as he suspected David wanted – to use David's white body for pleasure.

Chapter Eight

THE FALL OF NEW ORLEANS

The battle arena progressed south; in August, 1861, the North's Federal Army, under the command of General McDowell, and the Confederate Army, under General Beauregard, confronted one another at Springfield, Missouri; next followed McDowell's ill-fated siege of Lexington, and a subsequent battle at Leesburg, Virginia. The southern troops fought hard and were victorious. But despite the retreats which they forced upon the northern army during these months, Beauregard's losses were great and spirit was flagging. The two armies met again at Drainsville, Virginia, four days before Christmas, 1861, and the rebels scored another overwhelming victory along the banks of the Cumberland River in the state of Tennessee.

Winter snow and icy rains worsened conditions during the winter months of 1861–1862; journalists reported savage looting and plundering on both sides; northern newspapers chronicled the successes of McDowell's troops whereas in the south the public heard about the courage and valour of Beauregard's soldiers in grey. The American flag was hoisted over the Confederacy's Fort Pulaski in Savannah, Georgia, and provided first-hand proof to the southern populace that the Federal troops were securing a stronger foothold in the Confederacy. Then, the worst and most devastating defeat in the sixteen-month old war came with the bombardment of Forts Jackson and St Phillips on the Mississippi River. The city of New Orleans was left unprotected and the commanding general of New Orleans, Major General Lovell, evacuated his troops from the city before the Federal Navy sailed up the Mississippi, leaving the city under the control of the mayor; the citizens fell into hysteria; New Orleans literally lay at the mercy of the enemy.

But southern pride, always stronger in New Orleans than any other Confederate city, prompted the many citizens who remained in the city to accost – both verbally and physically – their northern conquerors in the streets. The Federal Army especially suffered attacks from women and it posted notices throughout the city stating that any female who conducted herself like a prostitute would be treated as such.

*   *   *

Vicky laughed when she read the announcement which the prostitute, Eunice, brought to her, the handbill declaring that females would be treated as whores; she crumpled the sheet of paper into a ball and tossed it onto the floor of her bedroom. She said to Eunice, standing dumbstruck at the foot of her bed, 'That's news? To be treated like a whore? Have you ever been treated like anything else in New Orleans?'

Eunice announced, 'I want to leave New Orleans. I want to go while the Yankees are still allowing people to evacuate.'

'You're stupid,' Vicky muttered, her face still unpainted, her hair not yet coiffed in her usual pile of curls. 'The money's just getting good.'

'It's not the money.'

'It's Catherine, isn't it? You and Catherine want to leave here together?'

Eunice nodded.

'Fine,' Vicky said with resignation. 'It's your life, but let me tell you this. Let me tell you that you and Catherine think life's hard as a whore. But being a whore is easy. Wait until you try being a dyke in the world! Have you ever thought of that? People understand whores. But your kind? Dykes? Perverts? Hell, now that won't be so easy.'

Eunice began to speak, to defend herself, but stopped.

'You're not slaves to me,' Vicky continued. 'You can go when you want. Do what you want to. You both have money and, when that runs out, you have your looks to rely on. I have no doubt you'll survive.'

'The important thing is to get out of New Orleans.'

Shaking her head, Vicky said, 'I still say you're both very stupid. Don't think those Dixie dollars will last long! Do you know how much a loaf of bread costs these days? Two hundred dollars! For one loaf of bread! Two hundred dollars! You don't know these things. You don't have to pay grocery bills. But take it from me, honey, you'll need Yankee money. Real stuff! None of that Confederate stuff.'

'We discussed all that.'

Vicky knew she would have no trouble replacing the two prostitutes; many young girls were available these days to work in the luxury – and safety – of Petit Jour. Nevertheless, Vicky had always felt loyalty toward any female who worked for her and said, 'Those pearls Alphonse St Cloude gave you. They're still in my drawer over there. Take them.'

'No, I don't want to be reminded of him.'

Eunice had been relieved months ago when Alphonse had suddenly stopped coming to Petit Jour, the evening last August when a black coachman had been accosted on Rampart Street for being a slave-runner.

'Hell, jewels are always more stable than money,'

Vicky advised from her bed. 'Alphonse's poor mother won't take them. He stole them from her. But she doesn't want to see them again because she says they only remind her of him. You and Catherine might as well have them for security.'

Shaking her head, Eunice insisted, 'Thank you, but, no. I don't want them either.' She moved toward the bed to give Vicky a farewell kiss on the cheek.

'Forget the goodbyes,' Vicky said, holding up one hand to Eunice. 'Just concentrate now on surviving in the world. You're going to discover that being a whore is the best training a person can get.'

Vicky remained in bed after Eunice had departed; she thought about the pearls, about Eunice declining them, about principles and honour; she wondered if she completely misunderstood what some people called 'ethics' or was everyone else just stupid?

Chloe lived in a dilapidated shack across Esplanade Ridge which had once belonged to her octoroon aunt; Chloe had refused to go back to Dragonard Hill after Bernard was arrested and not heard of again; Chloe knew that Alphonse had been responsible for the attack on the Negro coachman.

Vicky could not understand Chloe's decision. She thought, 'Chloe does not even know where her bastard son is. The poor little wretch is just torturing herself. She looks worse than a rat these days. She takes in laundry, has become a scrub woman living in near poverty, rather than return to the one man in the world who loves her.'

Vicky then thought of her father, of David, of Posey, of what life must be like on Dragonard Hill during the war. She and her father had never been in communication but, since the Yankees had conquered New Orleans, there was no way to get word to anybody except by sea.

Realizing the fruitlessness of worry, Vicky decided to

think constructively, to concentrate on her own life. She rang the crystal bell next to her bed and when the black maid, Frances, appeared, she ordered, 'Get me a Yankee officer's uniform.'

The request horrified the loyal black servant.

'Don't just stand there gawking, Frances! I need a Yankee uniform for the show. Hell, all our customers are Yankee, we might as well dress up our girls to please the men with good money.'

'Show tits inside Yankee clothes, Miss Countess, Mam?'

'Tits are tits, Frances.'

Twelve hours later, Vicky sat behind the thin gauze scrim in the upstairs theatre at Petit Jour, smiling as she watched the northern conquerors watching a white prostitute kneeling in front of a virile Negro; the towering Negro wore only the Yankee officer's coat, a sword in a scabbard strapped around his bare waist and a pair of knee-high black leather boots; the white prostitute rubbed her furry mid-section against the Negro's boots, slowly licking her tongue up the scabbard's cold steel as the Yankee soldiers called for her to reach for the Negro's semi-erect penis. 'His cock! Suck his cock! Forget about the sword and go for the cock!'

Vicky felt reassured that she understood warfare.

Book Two

TWO WORLDS

Chapter Nine

HAVANA

Juan Carlos Veradaga, lustrous black curls tumbling over his fine olive complexion and rich clothing hugging his athletic frame, returned to Cuba as a mourner, learning that his crippled father had died in Havana while he himself had been travelling in Europe, that he now was the sole beneficiary of the Veradaga fortune, the heir to a title bestowed upon his forebears by King Ferdinand VII, and the lord of Palacio Veradaga, located in the princely district of Jesu Maria which was set behind the yellow washed walls of Havana's fortified harbour.

Juan Carlos – or Juanito, as his father and close friends had addressed him since childhood – found Havana astir with talk of the American Civil War; the family's financial advisers had waited so long for the young Veradaga heir to return to Cuba and assume his hereditary duties that they could not respect his period of mourning, instead pressing him for details about how they should proceed with his father's ships – the Civil War had closed American ports.

Juan Carlos Veradaga, not a religious man, saw no reason to respect his mourning period if his dignified advisers ignored it; he consequently renewed old friendships with other young men in Havana, accepting invitations to suppers, attending balls, enjoying the late afternoon outings in Havana's Plaza des Armas where the city's fashionable society encircled the square on horseback, in carriages, or peered down at the passage of slowly moving traffic from their balconies.

Three years living in Madrid, extensive travels to Rome, Paris and other cities of Europe and long sojourn from Havana had sophisticated Juanito's vision of the world. But, nevertheless, he still enjoyed the afternoon parade around Plaza des Armas best of all the social pleasures available to him.

Juanito's companion today was Luis Cantanou, another young man in his mid-twenties who sat proud, tall, assured in the saddle as he rode his horse slowly round the square listening to Juanito telling stories of Spain, about life there compared to this small island in the Caribbean.

'We Cubans are dilettantes,'' Juanito said, above the steady clip-clop of horses' hooves. 'We babble about the American Civil War. But what do we do? Ride round and round the Plaza des Armas!'

'What else is there to do, Juanito?' Luis asked. 'This is not Spain. We do not have the navy of England. We are not peopled like Russia. This is Cuba! A land not even as big as Mexico.' He spat.

'Small but rich, Luis. Rich and hot,' Juanito dabbed at his brow with a lace kerchief. Then pushing the kerchief back into the ornately embroidered cuff protruding from his sleeve, he added, 'We Spaniards living in Havana suffer not only from torrid weather. But blood, too, Luis. Aya! Am I hot-blooded today!'

Juanito's mention of blood made Luis Cantanou fleetingly reflect on his friend's background, recall the rumours persisting in Havana that young Juan Carlos Veradaga was not of pure Spanish extraction, that his mother had been a light-skinned Negress, or a woman from one of Europe's northern countries. Gossip even circulated in Havana that the Condesa Veradaga had been an American adventuress who had abandoned her crippled husband when their son had been a mere infant.

Luis said, 'I do not mean to be disrespectful, Juanito. I do not intend to speak blasphemously during your period of mourning. But I am curious. Are those putas still sent to visit you during your siesta?'

'Si! I'm surprised you remember, muchacho!'

'Remember? How could I forget? You are the envy of every young man in the city! Who else had a father who sent prostitutes to him for enjoyment in the comfort of his own bedroom?'

'I am still not certain the girls came from my father,' Juanito confided to his friend. 'We never spoke of the women. My father never asked if I enjoyed them or not. But, yes, the girls still arrive at the Palacio every day like clockwork. They, in fact, began the very day I returned home from Madrid.'

The resumption of the arrangement intrigued Luis. He asked, 'Do you think it is part of your patrimony? To receive a new and different girl every afternoon for the rest of your life?'

Juanito answered, 'Every Spanish father wants his son to be virile. But I do not think my father's book-keepers and scribes would allow for such a perpetuity! They are obedient and trustworthy men. But to make arrangements for whores! Never!'

'You trust the accountants who run the business?'

'I look at the books every day. They dare not hide anything. I see what warehouses are full. How many slaves are sickly on the Finca.'

Furrowing his brow, Juanito said, 'I found out only today that we have one ship which is idle. A fine vessel called the *Pina*.'

'One ship! You are lucky, Juanito! The Sponteo family has their entire fleet in the locks! The Suarez family has not sent a ship to sea for a year. But you will hear all that tonight at the ball. The Suarez household has taken lately to complaining in public.'

'Of course. The Suarez ball. What does their young daughter look like these days?'

'Dina? She has changed much since you left for Madrid! I think she is about ready to fly from the coop!'

Juanito laughed. 'That old hen, Luisa Suarez, has probably not changed, though. More protective, more jealous, more guarding of Dina than ever, eh?'

'But Juanito, you are modest! Every family in Havana will try to match up you with their daughter!'

'No,' Juanito shook his head. 'It would be easy to love Dina. But I am not ready to settle down. I want . . .'

Juanito suddenly stopped when he saw a veiled woman drop a lace square on the cobblestones; he swung one leg over his saddle and, keeping his other boot in the stirrup, he scooped up the lace from the ground and flourished it toward the woman veiled in black.

'So gallant!' Luis praised as he and Juanito continued around the square. 'What did she look like under the veil? Could you see?'

'I could see she was an old lady,' Juanito answered, slightly disappointed. 'She was also dark. And there was something wrong with her skin.'

'A leper?' Luis laughed, saying, 'Trust my friend, Juanito, to play the caballero to a leper woman!'

'Do not make a joke,' Juanito spoke seriously, his handsome face was grave. 'This was not the first time I have seen that woman in Havana. I remember her from when I was a child. I guess some old ladies never die.'

'You saw her in a dream, muchacho. Now let us talk again about the putas.'

*　　*　　*

The black woman's name was Naomi; she did not consider herself old, nor did she think of herself as ugly, although the prune-coloured skin of her face was disfigured, pulled, stretched by burns, the battle-scars of a slave uprising on the island of St Kitts; Naomi wore her blemishes and age as proud badges of a woman who had loved, fought and waited for only one man in her long life.

Naomi, now standing inside the grillework fence centring the Plaza des Armas, watched Juanito and his friend disappear on horseback in the fashionable traffic; she held the lace square which Juanito had retrieved for her from the cobblestones.

Three years had passed since Naomi had last seen Juanito; the time had broadened his shoulders, given character to his face, made him into a man; old Conde Veradaga's death had also given Juanito a title and one of the country's largest fortunes.

Chuckling to herself, Naomi motioned for her own coachman to emerge from the portal across the square, to take her back to the district of Regla where she would choose another prostitute to send tomorrow afternoon to Juanito at Palacio Veradaga.

The resumption of old schedules, choosing girls again and sending them to Juanito during the siesta hour, excited Naomi. She enjoyed organizing the sexual lives of young men; her life had always been dedicated to providing pleasures, often perverse, frequently domineering or excessively passive, to men.

But Juanito's love-making did not include urges to dominate women, nor to have women dominate him; Naomi had learned from the prostitutes whom she secretly sent to Palacio Veradaga that Juanito was a basic sensualist, a man dissimilar from his most illustrious ancestor.

Naomi again smiled when she thought of Juanito's most famous progenitor, not the Conde Veradaga, but the Englishman, Richard Abdee, who had once been the public whipmaster on the island of St Kitts, a man who Juanito did not even know. Not yet.

Although Juanito showed none of Richard Abdee's taste for perverse sex, Naomi might soon see if the young heir had a taste for adventure. Abdee himself was interested in learning this fact; the renegade Englishman who had once been the 'dragonard' on St Kitts now enjoyed observing, receiving reports, watching the rise – or decline – of his progeny.

Naomi's black carriage bumped and rattled between the squalid buildings lining the streets of Regla, taking her back to Richard Abdee's slave house; Naomi and Abdee had a new plan concerning a ship, firearms and an adventure for young Juanito.

Chapter Ten

A GIRL CALLED TOMORROW

The tall iron gates of Palacio Veradaga remained shut
during the afternoon siesta; a black wreath of mourning still hung alongside the gateway's brass bell-chain –
but little else betrayed occupancy behind the thick stone
walls; the palace's louvred jalousies were pulled shut
against the hot Cuban sun and the leaves of banana trees
in the courtyard hung brown, limp, torn, undisturbed by
even the slightest ocean breeze.

The afternoon darkness within Juanito's bedroom was
cut by shafts of light slanting through the jalousies,
forming a regularity of stripes on the white marble floor;
a tall teakwood bed set on a dais in the centre of the
cavernous room; two bodies coupled together moved
quickly, in unison, on the white linen sheets. Juanito,
slim and sinewy with muscle, drove his virile thrusts
into a sylph-like creature with skin the colour of weak
tea; Juanito threw back his head, his glossy black ringlets
curled tightly with perspiration, and he drove harder as
he gasped louder, more satisfying, pushing, pulling his
thick phallus into the vagina rich with black wiry hair.

'Magnifico!' his love partner groaned as she tossed
her head on the mound of downy pillows. 'Magnifico,
muchacho! Muy magnifico!'

Juanito was oblivious to her praise, unnoticing of the
young woman's hands gently gripping his shoulders, her
thighs pressed open to receive his final drives of sexuality;
he held his thickly lashed eyelids shut and gasped as he

worked to drain the animal excitement from his phallus.

Finally, he collapsed onto the mattress alongside the slim young woman, realizing that she had also crested to an orgasm with him, that she rested alongside his body with equal satisfaction.

He whispered, 'What is your name?'

'Anna.'

'You have Indian blood in you, Anna,' he said, kissing one of her prominent cheekbones.

'Si, Indian,' she replied, then added, 'and Negro, and Spanish and Dutch, a little bit of English, some Danish, some Portuguese and, I think, a drop or two of Arab blood, too.'

'You are many things, Anna!' he said, grinning as he put his face alongside hers on the mattress.

'I have the blood of every nation which plundered the Caribbean.' She touched the tip of his nose with her finger, asking, 'What may I call you, Senor?'

'Juanito.'

'Juanito? But you are not little!'

'I was once.'

She said, 'But now you will only get bigger.'

'Do you want me bigger? Did I not satisfy you?'

'You are considerate, Senor Juanito. I am only a puta. But you are – '

'Shhh!' Juanito reached to press her lips shut, interrupting. 'You are a . . . princess!'

Kissing his fingers, Anna said, 'And you must not waste your time in Havana. Even with a princess. You must go out into the world, Senor Juanito.'

The words stunned Juanito, jolted him from the lull of their sexual wake. He pulled back his head, answering, 'What a curious thing to say to me, Princess Anna! Even impudent!'

'But I am a princess! You say so yourself. I can say

132

anything. Besides, why is it impudent to say you should travel?'

Juanito sat upright on the mattress and said, 'For your information, Princess Anna, I have just returned to Havana from Spain.'

The brown girl was not impressed. She replied, 'I do not mean you should travel to Spain! Not the old world! I mean America! There is a fortune waiting there.'

'Do you think I am a servant in this house, Princess Anna?'

'I say money has nothing to do with fortunes,' she argued, now also sitting up on the bed. 'That is what *I* say! I say you should enrich your life, Senor Juanito! Just think! You have one ship sitting idle in the harbour. Imagine the adventurous ways you can use it!'

'How do you know what I have in the harbour?' he asked, arching one eyebrow. 'Who are you really, my little Princess Anna?'

'I am ... Tomorrow!'

'Tomorrow?'

'That is what an Englishman calls me. An old Englishman and a black woman whose face has been burned badly by fire. I think the black woman is a witch. The Englishman and she are lovers. They have been for years. And they call me "Tomorrow" because of the blood in my veins. Does that make any sense to you, Senor Juanito?'

'Not really. But tell me more about them. The old Englishman and the black woman who you say is a witch."

Anna swung her bare feet across the side of the bed, answering, 'They believe the future of the world lies in the hands of people like me. I am sorry to say this but old families like yours – pure blood – are destined for doom. That is why it would be wise for you to enrich yourself in new ways. To go to a new world.'

'Is that your advice or theirs?' he asked sarcastically. 'Whose wisdom do I enjoy?'

'Does it matter where wisdom comes from?'

Still piqued by the girl and her story, he persisted, 'Who are they? This old Englishman and the black witch.'

The young prostitute shrugged. 'He is a slave dealer. She lives with him in an old building, a slave-house in the district of Regla.'

'Tell me his name. My father ran slaves, too. Perhaps I heard of this old Englishman who sleeps with black witches!'

'No. Not him. He has no friends. They seldom go out.'

'Then how do you know them?'

The girl reached for her clothing, a simple white cotton shift and woven leather sandals; she answered, 'I live near them in Regla.'

'Who sent you to me?' Juanito suddenly asked. 'Who sends all the other girls to me during my siesta? And do not say you don't know, little princess, or – ' he pulled back his hand in a mock threat.

Glaring up at him, she defiantly asked, 'Dare you strike Tomorrow, Senor?'

Releasing his grasp, Juanito said, 'You are a strange one! Calling yourself "Tomorrow". Knowing how many ships I have in the harbour. Telling me to go to America! I think you are the witch.'

'If that is so, why don't you ask me to tell you your future?'

'What *is* my future?'

'Guns!' she whispered, her black eyes widening. 'You will sail guns to America! In your ship, the *Pina*.' She then pulled an embroidered shawl around her head and moved quickly toward the tall, ornately carved door.

*   *   *

Juanito sat naked, stupefied, on the edge of the bed after Anna had departed from Palacio Veradaga; he considered the words she had told him, wondering how she possibly could have known about the *Pina*, his one ship to set at anchor in the harbour. Who was this Anna? Who had sent her to him? She had spoken, been more loquacious than any of the prostitutes who had ever visited him during the siesta hour. Why? And who was the old Englishman of whom Anna had spoken so fondly? The black witch he lived with? It was then, considering the slave-dealer who supposedly lived in the district of Regla with his ancient mistress, that Juanito remembered an incident from the Plaza des Armas, a woman who had dropped her lace kerchief to the cobblestones. Juanito recalled having gallantly retrieved the kerchief for the woman, but, when he had gazed through her veils, he had seen that her face was hideously scarred, deformed, mottled as if disfigured by severe burns. Was she the old Negress about whom Anna had spoken? The witch who lived with the English slave-dealer? Juanito definitely remembered having previously seen the same old Negress; he had seen her in Havana since he was a young boy. Did she follow him? Was she the one who sent prostitutes to him? Who was she? Was she really a witch, the crone who had dubbed Anna, the prostitute, 'Tomorrow' and believed that future control of the world lay with people of mixed blood? Was she also the one who now fore-saw Juanito's destiny involved running guns to America? Juanito did not believe in prophecy nor coincidences, but he definitely felt as if someone – or more than one person – was keeping him under an almost demonic surveillance. He felt displeased, even frightened. But also excited. Guns? Breaking a blockade? Yes, the prospect secretly thrilled him.

*　　*　　*

The crack of a long black leather whip echoed in the windowless room, deep within the Regla slave house; Naomi sat with Richard Abdee in the shadows watching a naked black man snap the whip over a white woman who knelt cowering, crying in front of him on the floor.

The woman's name was Teresa Calleja, the wife of a Mexican diplomat who had come to Havana to discuss Mexico's continuation of military protection for Cuba; Don Sancho Calleja also sat in the windowless room, watching his wife being debased by the Negro, a black man who was neither handsome nor important, merely a nameless male, endowed like a stallion, adept at overpowering women, at flailing a whip like a master; Don Sancho Calleja enjoyed the welcome extended to him in Richard Abdee's slave house in Regla, the one place where he could satisfy his desire to watch his young wife be debased like a whore, a bitch slave, a female far beneath her true social station.

Teresa Calleja also welcomed her visits to Havana; she had been raised in a Spanish convent, with skin as white as a nun, but she also possessed a shameless sexual hunger, a thirst for domination, to which few women confessed.

The sight of the domineering black man, the sound of the cruel whip, the knowledge that she was being observed — all these elements worked as a drug on the aristocratic Teresa Calleja.

She pleaded, 'Please . . . please, permit me to love you, sir!'

The Negro raised his bare foot, levelled his sole against

Teresa's face and pushed her down to the stone floor.

Teresa whimpered, wrapping her arms lovingly around the Negro's large foot, kissing its sole, curling around his other leg like a cat, rubbing her naked body against the cold stone floor.

Sancho Calleja, excited by watching this encounter, rose from his chair to goad the black man, 'Punish the bitch . . . she has disobeyed you . . . she has not cooked your supper . . . punish the lazy slave bitch . . .'

Teresa begged, 'Forgive me . . . I confess . . . I have been naughty . . . I did not do my work . . . I have only sat by the window all day waiting for you to come home and make love to me . . .' She reached toward the Negro's limp penis.

'See!' her husband taunted. 'See, you bitch! You do not even arouse him! You do not even make his cock hard! Why should he allow you the privilege even to . . . lick it?'

'I want to suck it!' Teresa wailed. 'I want to take him in my mouth . . . to clean his cock with my tongue . . . please, master, sir . . .'

The whip snapped again in the air; Teresa fell to her face on the floor, raising her pink buttocks as a target; then, the whip came down once, twice, three times across her tender skin; she screamed; her husband backed away, rubbing his phallus inside his breeches as he watched the black man make a ladder of blood up Teresa's slim back.

Naomi waited until both Sancho and Teresa Calleja had both reached their orgasms before she sent the virile Negro from the room; she ordered robes to be brought to her Mexican guests, then motioned for them to come and sit beside her and Richard Abdee in the tall leather-armed chairs in the opposite corner of the windowless room.

Richard Abdee remained sitting in shadows; his voice was thin, emotionless, but, nevertheless, a voice of assurance; he said, 'I want to speak about guns. Rifles. Enough weapons to make a shipment to New Orleans.'

'Does senor have a ship?' Calleja asked, keeping his eyes lowered, masturbation having sobered his spirits.

'A young Cuban I know has a ship,' Abdee answered. 'He shall be given your name. You will approach him. But you shall not drive a hard bargain with him, Senor Calleja.'

'When will this happen, Senor?' Calleja mopped his brow, glancing quickly at his wife. 'We must soon return to Mexico.'

'Soon,' Abdee said. 'In good time.'

Chapter Eleven

SURVIVORS

Vicky did not care what people thought about the way in which she ran her bordello during the Federal Army's occupation of New Orleans. As the first gruelling months passed into a year and then, as 1863 wore to a bitter close, Vicky continued to do what she wanted, welcoming whoever had the necessary money to visit her establishment; she doubled-up girls in their rooms to make space for Northern soldiers demanding to be billeted in the occupied city; she made the most uncouth soldier welcome in Petit Jour; Creole society, of course, stopped coming to the bordello on Rampart Street but Vicky still ran the most popular house of vice in the city, Yankee officers literally pulling rank on conscripted troops to live at the house of 'Condesa Veradaga'.

The theatre remained intact on the bordello's top floor; Vicky no longer showed dramatic sketches of black people in servitude to whites; she avoided the subject of racial slavery; she dressed her players in Yankee blue uniforms, banishing Dixie grey from her premises; she chose patriotic Northern themes – the Boston Tea Party, the signing of the Declaration of Independence, General Washington's historic crossing of the River Delaware—as subjects for her erotic entertainments; she painstakingly played each tableau for sexual innuendo, carefully avoiding any sensitive political overtures, making American heroes such as Benjamin Franklin, Thomas Jefferson, Davey Crockett, into overtly masculine caricatures, even inducing young, awkward Yankee soldiers to appear in situations with her prostitutes, clever vignettes which amused, entertained, even titillated their senior officers. Vicky taught a bumbling Pennsylvania farmboy how to stand like a majestic Adonis over two servile prostitutes; she coached a clerk from New York City and a school boy from Baltimore how to make love – as father and son – to Dolly Madison; she blocked the small candle-lit stage like a professional manager for five naked men wearing racoon hats to repel the attack of seven prostitutes representing a band of renegade Indians, but the buxom women were adorned with colourful maribou feathers rather than eagle, turkey and other wildfowl feathers usually attributed to Indians. Thus Vicky bravely faced the occupation of New Orleans; she avoided the streets more than before, knowing she would be mobbed by angry citizens as a Yankee sympathizer; she remained locked inside her bordello determined to earn every Federal dollar carried through her front door; she knew now for certain that Confederate money was doomed; she recognized that her survival was dependent on money and, unashamedly, Vicky embraced all facets of whoredom. Amongst them was included the taking of General William Turkel from Burkeston, Massachusetts, as her lover.

*   *   *

Chloe St Cloude survived in New Orleans too, but not in the style nor with the bravado of Vicky; Chloe kept close to the small wooden house located in Faubourg Maurigny across Esplanade Ridge. She did not respond to the letters which Peter Abdee managed to have delivered at the riverside cottage; she sat late at night reading and re-reading Peter's pleas for some news of her, implorations, that if she were alive, to return to him and Dragonard Hill.

Disappointment in the son which she had borne for Peter Abdee burdened Chloe more than the chores she performed to eke out a livelihood in New Orleans; Chloe laundered and mended sheets; she swept streets, cared for children and, without pay, she attended the sickly and wounded in the military hospital recently established on Canal Street.

But Alphonse remained Chloe's millstone; she saw his past weakness of character as her own betrayal to Peter Abdee; she interpreted his chicanery as bad blood which she herself had brought to the union she had once so tenderly enjoyed at Dragonard Hill; she multiplied her misery by suffering from guilt, by thinking how she had given birth to Alphonse out of wedlock and not providing him with a proper home and a sound start in the world.

Alphonse and Chloe had not spoken since he had left Dragonard Hill. The theft of the jewellery no longer mattered to Chloe. It had become minor compared to stories she had heard whispered about evil deeds which her son had done, that he had been responsible for Bernard's arrest, that he had been spreading malicious rumours about David Abdee and Abolitionist activity at Dragonard Hill.

Chloe did not know Alphonse's whereabouts; she had not heard any recent stories about him in New Orleans. From the earlier rumours she feared that his bitterness had taken an evil turn, and she was certain that he was not dead, but lurking somewhere in the world waiting to cause trouble for the Abdee family. Chloe blamed herself for all these things, her soul suffering as much as her physical health.

*　　　*　　　*

Peter Abdee received official notice at long last from the North's headquarters in New Orleans about Bernard's arrest and execution for treason; he interpreted it as one more sign of the Yankees strengthening foothold in the South and the futility of protesting; he devoted himself to pursuing plantation life as best he could in the Louisiana wilderness despite the restrictions put on agriculture by military changes; he stored his cotton crops in plantation warehouses instead of sending wagons to New Orleans as he had done in the past; an embargo had been placed on all Confederate exports; cotton, sugar, tobacco, all produce rotted in the fields and many fields were planted with salt by Southerners who did not want Yankee invaders – or Negroes – to reap future harvests.

During this second year of wartime, Peter Abdee allowed his people on Dragonard Hill and Greenleaf Plantation more time to cut and mill timber, to make repairs on their living quarters, construct new ones, to plant, harvest and preserve food for themselves.

As before, the months of autumn remained a time for the preparations of winter. But now that a war was being waged to emancipate slaves, Peter Abdee knew that other preparations must be made for the future.

Peter Abdee feared the prospects of the Confederacy's slave population receiving their freedom but having no means of livelihood to support themselves in the world once they were liberated; he himself had freed slaves in the past and knew the responsibilities of bestowing freedom on men, women, families who possessed no idea about survival in the world.

When Negro men were eventually conscripted into battle, Peter Abdee did not rejoice but recognized a perverse step forward made in the cause of freedom; military conscription had a slow but positive effect on the bigotry of white people; masters and slaves fought, if not as equals, then at least, in the same arena : the unfortunate spilling of blood led to a democracy.

David Abdee joined the Louisiana Seventh Battalion in June, 1863; his decision to fight for the Confederacy was more academic than patriotic. David's conversation with his father on the evening before his departure from Dragonard Hill hedged between humour and melancholy.

Sitting in the chair across the fireplace from his father in the firelit parlour at Dragonard Hill, David joked, 'My time was running out. I had to join before they started recruiting women, children and dogs who can walk on their hind-legs.'

Peter was more serious. He confided, 'David, I still believe you could serve the Confederacy better at home than on a battlefield.'

'But I am not fighting for the Confederacy! I believe we are wrong! I'm going only to protect our land. I'm the Abdee token. I'm tossing myself into the hat of public approval.' David swirled the golden brandy in his glass, continuing, 'But, what we and our neighbours are going to do with our land without slaves, I don't know . . .'

He lifted his head and said bluntly, 'But let's face it, father. You have as much guilt about slavery as I do.'

Peter answered, 'I inherited this land from the Selby family. When I married Melissa. I also had to inherit the work force which toiled it. Slavery is part of the south's system. Black people are our tools.'

'Is that why you never married Chloe? Because of her colour?'

'Marriages of mixed blood trouble me, yes.'

'Have you heard from her, father? Has Chloe ever written to you?'

'No. She's probably still in New Orleans. That seems to be the place where everyone goes when they leave Dragonard Hill.'

143

'That's not true. Veronica went north.'

'With my blessing,' Peter said, then explained. 'I meant her sister, Vicky. She also ran away to New Orleans.' He did not elaborate. He kept secret, even repressed all he had ever learned about his daughter, Victoria.

David asked, 'Does it bother you that I have not produced heirs for you, father?'

'The Abdees are not a great family, David. Great, no; destructive, yes. Perhaps it is best we do not continue.'

'Where is your father?'

'Hell or the Caribbean. One's the same as the other.'

'You say that with so little compassion,' David Abdee himself spoke more authoritatively since he had decided to join the Confederate forces; also, his recent rediscovery of sexuality had given him confidence, a masculine presence previously not evident in his manner.

Peter answered, 'My father was not a compassionate man. Not from what I understood of him.'

'You never met him?'

'No. I don't even remember my mother. She fled from my father before I was born. Richard Abdee was a cruel, ambitious, selfish Englishman who emigrated to the West Indies. He married my mother, a Frenchwoman, for her plantation, a place called Petit Jour on the north end of the island of St Kitts. My mother abandoned St Kitts, leaving my father with his mistress, a black woman named Naomi. My mother took a few possessions and travelled with her maid, Ta-ta, and a son sired by my father. My mother died shortly after my birth, after the ship on which she was travelling had to put ashore somewhere along East Florida.'

David knew these stories; he also knew it pained his father to speak of them, of how Ta-ta had raised him, how her own son from Richard Abdee had challenged

Peter to a duel, a struggle which proved fatal for the half-caste young man whose name had been Monk.

David swigged down the brandy and, setting the glass on the table, he asked, 'Why do you not go after Chloe, Father?'

'I do not believe in chasing love, David,' Peter answered from his chair. 'Love goes where it is sent.'

David Abdee parted after this exchange with his father; he bade farewell to Posey in the kitchen annex, taking yet another letter which Posey had written to Veronica, and then David rode to Greenleaf to say good-bye to Maybelle and Ham and to ask one last favour of Tim.

*   *   *

David Abdee's request both flattered and perplexed Tim. David had told Tim that he feared that his father was quickly becoming old and, that if he should not return from the war, he wanted Tim to protect this land; David explained to Tim how Ham and Maybelle would obviously remain in stewardship of Greenleaf – provision was even made for them to inherit the plantation if Peter Abdee died – but David specifically asked Tim to watch over Dragonard Hill, explaining to him that he was younger, stronger, more fit to accept the responsibility of overseeing the larger plantation.

Tim said, 'My Ma and Pa – you forget. Black people cannot inherit property.'

'Perhaps not in the old world, Tim, but in the new world, we will all be astounded at what strange events can and will happen. Just promise me that you will watch over Dragonard Hill.'

Tim, putting his hand on David's thin shoulder, said, 'I promise.'

David said, 'You know I have always loved you, Tim.'

'I know.'

'More than a brother,' David's new honesty surprised even himself.

'I know,' Tim answered, trying to hold David's gaze.

'My father said a strange thing to me, Tim, before I left him. He said, "Love goes where it is sent". It was never sent to me.'

Tim chose to ignore the comment and, instead, patted David's shoulder, saying, "Don't worry about Dragonard Hill. I will protect it.'

David Abdee thus departed from his father's land, leaving more perplexed than ever by the mysteries of love. He lay with black women but why did he only feel genuine compassion for Tim? He wished he could give him much more than Greenleaf or Dragonard Hill.

Chapter Twelve

'YOUR SERVANT, X MISS POSEY'

Dear Miss Veronica — I write to you but I do not know if my letters get to you and your dear family. Miss Chloe went to New Orleans almost three years ago and never came back home. I have to wait for the nigger Von to drive the wagon to Carterville to take my letters to you. How are you? We are fine. Your father is fine. Master David is fine. He went to war and is master of many soldiers. He misses home. He writes letters to us and says he needs new leather boots and your father sent them to him. Do you still miss home? Last week five men came to the new house and took some red hens and two milk cows. Maybelle walked here from Greenleaf and tells us that men took cows horses and chickens from there. Maybelle says Yankees treat niggers same as dumb white trash around here and she says maybe she will not go north where you live even if she does get the chance. I get up in the morning same as usual when the sky is still black but I can now smell summer in the air and I know that soon the trees down by the old house will be big as a lettuce head. We all hope no worms get in the berry patch this year but your father tells me I worry too much about everything. I do worry a lot dear Miss Veronica. I worry for you and your dear family. You do not write letters telling your father about Miss Lindy, your dear Master Peter Mark and young Master Max. Are they in the big war too? I do not mean Miss Lindy. I know she is a fine lady and I hope she still has her good job teaching children at that red brick school house you wrote us about two years ago before this awful trouble started and you stopped writing. I do also worry about Miss Chloe. She is a very good teacher but she does not write to us from New Orleans where she must still be living if she is not dead. Poor thing. This is a bad letter but I know you will forgive me because I only want to say no more than hello from your old home and your dear loving father. I am your servant X Miss Posey.

Dear Miss Veronica – Today is hot as ten ovens full of pitch pine but we hope the rains do not start no more like we had last month. Your father feels much better now and wants to ride in the buggy to Greenleaf for fresh air. He says he is too old to go around the country on a horse. I say he is right about that. I do not say he is old. I say he is right not to go alone on a horse because we do not have worms this summer in the berry patch but we have local patrollers plus plenty of Yankees to make up for no worms. Some folks say they are not Yankees but southern boys and I think they tell lies. Who else could they be? I think there must be white trash people where you live same like we have white trash down here and they must not have money to put in the bank where your dear husband works for so many years and that is why they don't know you. No letters from Master David since he sent us a big long letter from Georgia. He is good about writing and makes his father very happy. Your father loves you very much and loves getting letters I know for a fact. He tells me not to fret about soldiers coming to spook me and make fun. He tells me to say I am a grand-mother and I am to hold up both hands and say I have ten fingers worth of grand-children living in Boston and that no Yankee soldiers will make trouble for me. Oh I do laugh when I sit alone here in the kitchen and think about me telling those stories. Ha. Ha. Miss Chloe would she laugh with me. Ha. Ha. I miss Miss Chloe but no more than your father misses that dear little thing. I do know your father would like getting a letter from her. Your father likes getting letters from his loved ones and your father loves you best of all. I give butter and apricot jam to the nigger Von who still takes my letters to the mail bag in Carterville. Do not forget that I can read and write. So I can read your letters to your dear father if you write here and tell us everything about you, your dear husband, Miss Lindy, Masters Peter Mark and Max. Please give them hello from your servant X Miss Posey.

Dear Miss Veronica – Your dear father tells me today that letters which do not get taken to a house are returned back to this house. I write this letter as a test to see if it comes back to me so I will keep it short and not waste paper. I am your servant X Miss Posey.

Dear Miss Veronica – My test letter did not come back to me so I know for a fact that you do get my letters. When you write to me to tell me for sure you have been getting my letters I will write back to you and tell you what happened to the porch at the old house. You will be very surprised. Your father says we should pull the old house down and use the boards to make more houses for niggers in the back hills where no green cotton is planted this year. Your father spends his days making big plans for niggers. Do not ask him about the old house porch when you do write us a letter some day. I know you love your home so I know you will be interested to know about soldiers coming to the house to take away

guns. I do not understand many things. I do not under-
stand why our soldiers take away most of our guns and
swords for themselves to use. What are we to protect us
with? But at least the scum patrollers had to give up some
of their guns to our soldiers too. I do not feel so good.
Your dear father tells me I miss people to cook for. He
eats my cooking but he is just one man all by himself. I
think maybe your dear father would like to hear from
you and your dear children very soon. I know you will
write a letter because your father loves you dear Miss
Veronica the best of anybody. I am your faithful servant
X Miss Posey.

*   *   *

Alphonse St Cloude held Posey's latest letter to
Veronica in one hand and a smile slowly spread across
his face; he reached for a tumbler of whisky and, bracing
himself with the rough liquor against the autumn chill of
Montgomery, Alabama, Alphonse put the letter with
other correspondence he had intercepted at the Confederate Postal Bureau.

Alphonse had come to Montgomery from New Orleans,
renting a room on State Street in a boarding-house where
Confederate Government employees also resided.

Montgomery had been chosen as the seat of the Confederacy when Jefferson Davis had been named its president in 1861. Davis had made his home – 'the White
House' – the headquarters there and, now, three years
later, an increasing number of bureaus and ministries
were centred in Montgomery, amongst them being the
postal centre to which all letters and parcels were routed,
particularly correspondence addressed to northern des-
tinations.

Alphonse befriended, drank and gambled with government employees; he made a comfortable living at the gaming tables, pitting himself against innocent young white men, gleaning information as he played roulette and cards, allowing losers to postpone payment of debts when they were forthcoming with information he wanted. He had quickly discovered about the Confederate postal service, learning that leather mail bags arrived weekly in Montgomery from all points within the Confederacy.

The latest mail bag from northern Louisiana had been delivered to the Postal Bureau this morning. Alphonse found the pouch from Carterville, Louisiana and quickly searched amongst the letters for names and addresses familiar to him. He found Posey's latest letter to Veronica and, putting it into his pocket, he returned to his room on State Street.

Alphonse already knew many details which Posey mentioned in letters to Veronica. He knew that Peter Abdee was sickly, that David Abdee had gone to war, that Federal troops were confiscating farm goods and the Confederates were supplementing their quickly dwindling artillery with guns taken from other Southerners. He also knew that his mother, Chloe St Cloude, had remained in New Orleans.

In passing months Alphonse had gleaned his information about Dragonard Hill through the network of Southern patrollers, an organization of men too old to fight, farmers and residents of small towns who wanted to perform some patriotic war duty.

Billy Cramer was the chief patroller from Carterville in northern Louisiana; he kept in communication with the Patrol Federation in the capital of Montgomery. Alphonse knew that Cramer and his friends in Troy were still suspicious of him, even after Alphonse's new friends in various military departments had vouched for his dependability, had cited Alphonse's bravery for pointing out an Abolitionist slave-runner in New Orleans before the occupation of the city.

Also, Alphonse knew that patrollers in Carterville and Troy were too bigoted to trust a gens de couleur libre. But he further realized that the northern Louisiana patrollers loathed Peter Abdee as much as he himself did, that the redneck farmers would do anything to settle old scores with the Abdee family.

Alphonse sat in his room on State Street and debated about immediately sending a telegram to Troy to inform Billy Cramer that he had just received incriminating evidence against Dragonard Hill.

But listening to the cold rain beat against the window pane, Alphonse again studied Posey's childlike printing and thought how he should make certain that he had ample evidence to destroy the Abdee family and their arrogant slaves.

Alphonse reached for his whisky; he took a long swig and, then removing the same type of vellum paper and lead pencil which Posey had used writing his letters to Veronica, Alphonse lowered his head to the table and began to write.

Dear Miss Veronica – Another letter arrived today by secret messenger from Boston. Your poor father is so pleased to hear that you and your dear husband are willing to help him sneak out good niggers from here and fool those stupid white trash patrollers. I know the underground railway is really not a train but a way for decent people like you and your family to trick dumb cluck white trash like Billy Cramer in Troy ...

Chapter Thirteen

THE PATROLLERS

Tim was becoming increasingly concerned about his mother and father's safety at Greenleaf as white southerners were gradually beginning to accept the fact that the North might possibly win America's Civil War and all Negro slaves would be emancipated from their life-long bondage.

It was no secret that many white people in the neighbourhood resented Ham and Maybelle living comfortably at Greenleaf, existing better than many white farmers and residents of the nearby towns of Troy and Carterville. Tim made as many trips to Troy as plantation work allowed him; he tried to gather what information he could during those visits, learning what he could about the war's progress, current political news and, most important, the town's opinion about his master, Peter Abdee.

It was no lie that many white people could not tell one Negro from another; this inability amused Tim but he also used it as a way to linger near the general store, moving and lazily adjusting hemp bags in the bed of the wagon in order to eavesdrop on conversations between local white men.

Young Sebbie had ridden into Troy with Tim today but Sebbie sat on the ground, leaning against one of the wagon's large wooden wheels, stealing glances at a red-haired white woman who was waiting by herself in a wagon parked across the dirt street. This pleased Tim because the white men's conversation was about the war and he preferred that Sebbie did not hear it, that everyone at Greenleaf and Dragonard Hill forgot about war and, especially, the guns stolen from the soldiers' pack train by The Pothole.

Tim pushed another bag across the wagon's splintery bed and strained to hear the words of a man whose name he knew was Billy Cramer.

*   *   *

Billy Cramer, a big-bellied man who swaggered when he walked and sat with his hirsute chest expanded when he sank down to a chair, enjoyed the role of Chief Patroller of northern Louisiana, a position of high local esteem.

Cramer sat on the general store's porch this morning bragging about receiving a cable from Montgomery, Alabama, a telegraphed message from the Confederacy's capital.

He announced to the other balding and white-haired men lounging around his chair on the splintery wooden porch, 'This time it sounds like we're in for some trouble.'

Cramer's one outspoken rival in Troy was Burt Thomas, a wiry old man with a mouth full of silver teeth. He spat onto the dirt road, considered Cramer's announcement and asked, 'Who sent the message to you, Billy? General Beauregard himself? Waiting for you to come to Montgomery and tell him how to win the war?'

'Sarcasm's no good in a time like this, Burt. We white folk around here got to rally together.'

'We white folks has got to get us some guns!' Burt Thomas grunted. 'It's one thing our men confiscating our guns for soldiers to use. We ain't got no armaments factories down here to keep up the supply. But it's another thing stripping us patrollers nearly bare of artillery when we might be needing to do some protecting.'

A chorus of approval greeted Burt Thomas's opinion; the Confederacy's recent appropriation of excess firearms had angered many local citizens, especially the men too old to join the war but who still felt a patriotic urge to kill, plunder and lay waste in the name of their homeland.

Billy Cramer, anxious to regain attention, tipped his chair back on its back legs and announced, 'The telegram was about old man Abdee and all those nigger lovers at Dragonard Hill.'

The men stared at Cramer and then looked at one another. Thomas asked, 'What about them? Abdee had to give up guns same as us.'

'The telegram wasn't about guns, for Christ's sake,' Cramer sneered. 'If you shut your trap for a while about guns and let me tell about them Abdees being slaverunners – '

'Slave-runners?'

Cramer nodded, saying, 'You've heard about the underground railway?'

'That Abolitionist network? Sure we have,' Thomas said.

Tapping the chest pocket of his blue cambric shirt, Cramer said, 'I got me proof. Proof right here that old man Abdee's daughter in Boston is helping him run slaves to the North.'

'Then why don't Montgomery send soldiers here to stop it?' Thomas demanded. 'Arrest the sneaking nigger lovers.'

Billy Cramer chewed on a wooden toothpick, calmly answering, 'Soldiers too busy fighting war, ain't they? Government has to depend on other people.'

'Meaning you?' Thomas asked.

'Me, you, every respectable southerner.'

'What's headquarters say to do?' Thomas pressed.

Billy Cramer, unwilling to admit the telegram was unofficial, realizing that Burt Thomas would scoff at him for listening to Peter Abdee's half-caste son, answered, 'We must act as we see fit. This is time of war.'

'How we going to act with no guns? No ammunition?'

One angered farmer suggested, 'I got a squirrel gun and a few mighty strong birch clubs.'

'Whips!' said a second farmer.

'They fight back!' Burt Thomas said.

'Not if we lock the whole kit and caboodle in a pen!' Billy Cramer said, sneering triumphantly at Burt Thomas. 'Like the Army do with Yankee prisoners. Pull a few in at a time. Make a few night raids. Start maybe at Greenleaf and then work our way over to Dragonard Hill . . .'

Tim walked slowly around the wagon, kicked Sebbie to climb up in the seat, and casually unknotted the team's leather reins. He knew it was unwise to wait to hear more.

*   *   *

Maybelle, her eyes rounded with disbelief, listened to Tim repeat the story about the white patrollers running night raids on Greenleaf and Dragonard Hill plantations, imprisoning Negroes as a retaliation against the Abolitionist activity in the neighbourhood.

'You mean to say they wants to lock us in like cows? Put us all in a corral?' Maybelle stood on the back steps of Greenleaf, looking down at Tim still dusty from the public road.

'That's what they talking, Ma,' Tim answered.

'But we ain't done nothing!' Maybelle wailed. 'What we done?'

'They scared of Master Peter setting us loose.'

'That's crazy! Them no good white trash patrollers just needs to come here and see all the cabins Master Peter's building for niggers. No man who builds cabins is planning to set nobody loose!'

'But that Billy Cramer,' Tim proceeded, 'he said he got proof about Miss Veronica being involved. He said he got a telegram from Montgomery.'

'Now that's a lie if I ever heard one! I know for a fact Miss Veronica ain't planning nothing with her daddy. Miss Posey is moaning and complaining all the time about Miss Veronica not answering – '

Maybelle stopped. She said, 'I hope that that Miss Posey ain't done nothing stupid. She brags about writing letters to Boston. I hope she ain't done written nothing that somebody else laid their no good hands on.'

'No good complaining about Posey, Ma,' Tim said. 'What's done's done. We got to start thinking of protecting ourselves.'

'What can we do?' Maybelle wailed. 'There's nothing niggers can do against crazy men like Billy Cramer and those old duffers in Troy! Not when they get people all riled up against us!'

'Yes, there is something we can do, Ma,' Tim calmly said. 'They ain't got guns.'

'So what? Who does?'

'Me.'

Maybelle stared at him.

'I got guns, Ma.'

'You?'

He nodded.

'Guns?' The word was whispered. 'You got guns, boy?'

'Guns and ammunition.'

'Where you get guns, boy? What you done bad to

get guns, boy? Tim, if you done something stupid that's going to get you skinned alive, get you killed, you better start running. You better start running through them trees because – '

'Ma, you calm yourself. You've got to help me. You be the only smart person I know. You got to help me make a plan to protect us.'

'But we just niggers, boy!' Maybelle insisted, wringing the apron in her hands. 'We just niggers they want to herd like cattle!'

'That's our advantage now, Ma. White men don't suspect a few poor niggers got . . . guns.' Tim's eyes gleamed; his teeth shone white as he smiled.

'Don't look like that, boy. Don't look like that. It scares me.'

'This ain't no time to be scared, Ma. This is a time to use your head and be strong. You be a clever gal so I'm looking to you to help to protect Greenleaf and Dragonard Hill. Think you can do it?'

Maybelle, holding her son's eyes, slowly nodded her head, saying, 'I helps you, boy. I helps you and anybody else it takes to protect our home.'

Tim then explained who else knew about the guns, where they were hidden, how he had painstakingly kept them oiled and the ammunition dried, the way they must decide was best to protect such a large territory.

*　　*　　*

Sebbie jubilantly raced in the darkness along the public road that night, eager to share with Loraine the secret of seeing one another in Troy that afternoon and no one realized they knew one another.

But Sebbie found Loraine trembling in the cottonwoods near her cabin; their meeting had been prearranged and anticipated by both but Loraine resisted Sebbie's warm embraces, saying, 'I must stop seeing you.'

'Why must you stop seeing me? Everybody saw us both in town today and nobody guessed . . . or did they?'

Loraine shook her head. 'No, but it is too dangerous. Especially now.'

'Why now?'

'You are from Greenleaf.'

Sebbie nodded. He had never tried to keep any secrets from Loraine in the many months and passing seasons they had managed to meet for love-making; Loraine never spoke about herself but Sebbie was prepared to tell her everything about himself. He knew it was useless to pretend he was anything but a slave; he knew that Loraine had begun seeing him to ease her sexual frustrations and, in their secret meetings, she had come to need and depend on the satisfaction he gave to her.

'It's my husband,' she whispered. 'He's older than me. Also, Billy hates your master something awful.'

'Master Peter? Your husband knows Master Peter?'

'Not as a friend. My husband is the head of the patrollers in Troy. I know there might be trouble soon – '

Stopping herself, Loraine said, 'I mustn't talk out of place. Billy would kill me and you if he knew we met like this. He's a mighty proud man and if word got out that "Billy Cramer's wife" was seeing a . . .'

'Nigger,' Sebbie said, wrapping his arm around her. 'Don't be afraid to say it. I ain't ashamed.'

Sinking her head against his shoulder, she said, 'You are so young but sometimes you be so much smarter than all the older people I know. Especially me. Oh, I'm so stupid, so danged stupid to keep seeing you like this . . .'

'You enjoys me.' Sebbie was working his hand down Loraine's back, nibbling at her ear, taking her hand and resting it between his legs, making her fingers squeeze his manhood which he knew she had come to crave.

Loraine did not resist his dominant way with her, allowing him to pull her closer towards him without a struggle, permitting him to run his hand inside her dress and finger the moisture between her legs.

Sebbie whispered, 'Your pretty's ready for me. I feels it boiling.'

'I'm always ready for you.'

'You going to suck me?'

'Suck you till you got no juice left in your big beautiful black pecker.'

'You loves me?' he asked, working her hand back and forth on his erect penis.

'I loves you. Craves you. Needs you.'

'Then why you fighting me?'

'I ain't fighting you. I just knows we be risking . . .'

'Shhh,' Sebbie whispered, falling on top of Loraine's quivering body, excited to make love to this white woman who treated him – a slave – like her master.

Loraine lay with her legs curled around Sebbie's hard muscled thighs, cradling him as he drove into her, trembling silently as he pursued his lust with her.

Sebbie ran one hand through her red hair, fingering the rosy bud on her milky white breast with his other large black hand. The fact that her husband was Billy Cramer, the head patroller from Troy, strangely added to the excitement of this dangerous meeting. Sebbie knew that he would not stop seeing Loraine.

Chapter Fourteen

THEATRE OF SIN

Weaponry became a vital issue not only in the hinterlands of the Confederacy but also in cities and coastal zones and, by the end of 1863, the men of acclaim were captains and ship-owners who, either for profit or patriotism, braved the Federal Navy's blockade lining the South's Atlantic coastline and fanned across the Bay of Mexico.

New Orleans remained an occupied city but its citizens secretly celebrated a foreigner who had smuggled a shipload of rifles, pistols and muskets into the Louisiana swampland for the use of the Confederate Army.

The first stories to circulate in the French Quarter of New Orleans about the adventurer was that he was Cuban and, then, later, it became known that the brave stranger was not only young and handsome but also rich and titled; Creole hostesses vied to entertain him in their ancestral homes; his name was Conde Juan Carlos Veradaga.

Juan Carlos – or Juanito – did not learn until after five days in Louisiana that there was another person named Veradaga living in New Orleans. He learned the startling news as he sat in the sunny courtyard of Bernadot's Absinthe House on Toulouse Street in the French Quarter; he looked indignantly at the man seated across the round marble table from him. The man, a Confederate officer dressed in civilian clothes, apologetically explained. 'I merely said, Conde Juan Carlos, that there is a woman in this city known by the same name as yours. I meant no offence to you nor your family when I said she was a . . . whore. The Condesa Veradaga is notorious. She's no favourite of us Creoles. Her bordello is a virtual nest of Yankee activity – '

'Veradaga? It is impossible! No member of my family lives in this city. Impossible!'

Juanito had told few people about his true identity; one of the few was this afternoon's drinking companion, Lieutenant Phillip Balfour, who had paid him in gold for the arms shipment on behalf of the Confederacy.

Lieutenant Balfour leaned across the table, struggling to correct his social blunder. He whispered, 'Please forgive me, Conde Juan Carlos. The vile woman has obviously usurped your honourable name. But, please, pay no heed to such impudence. This city is famous for brazen women. Let us speak instead about you. I know you will soon leave New Orleans and return to Havana. An act which I consider to be wise. But I personally wish you could remain longer in this city. I would like to know more about you. Why you decided to help the Confederacy cause. How you came in possession of the arms. Why you, a Spanish nobleman – '

Juan Carlos sat stiffly on his chair in the courtyard and answered, 'Our agreement included no one asking me questions, Senor.'

Nodding, Lieutenant Balfour said, 'I stand corrected. I appreciate your risk. But please understand that I also am at risk by being in this city. I am a Confederate officer. New Orleans is now held under Federal Law.'

Juanito asked, 'And you say this "Condesa Veradaga" entertains Yankees in her house?'

'Entertains them?' Balfour threw back his head and laughed. 'Top ranking officers are billeted there. They literally make their home in that bordello called Petit Jour. They fight amongst themselves to live on Rampart Street with that bogus Condesa Veradaga.'

'Rampart Street? That is only a short distance from this very spot?'

Balfour understood the young Cuban's question. He warned, 'You must not consider going near that place, Conde Juan Carlos. It is too dangerous for you. True, only a few loyal Confederates know your identity. Our people have pawned their heirlooms to pay for the guns you brought to us. But we must always be careful of spies. You would be hanged if it were discovered that you ran a Yankee barricade with your ship.'

Juan Carlos held his head high, his nostrils flaring, as he said, 'Sir, a man who breaks naval barriers does not shrink from entering a bordello.'

'I do not mean to offend you. But I seem to be doing nothing else this afternoon. Please forgive me.'

Patting the Creole's hand, Juan Carlos said, 'You are the one who must forgive me. My nerves are on edge, I have not had much sleep since I arrived here. New Orleans is occupied by Northern vandals, si, but I have been entertained well in your city since my arrival. I have been treated like a hero – '

'But you *are* a hero, Conde Veradaga! And the stories whispered about you, mon Dieu!'

'Do not believe stories, Lieutenant. They usually are not true.' Juan Carlos paused, thinking of the stories which he himself had learned during the last two years in Havana, tales told to him in bits and pieces, information about his past which led him to realize that he was more – or perhaps less – what he believed himself, his father, his mother, his ancestry to be.

Juan Carlos had heard rumours in Havana about his shadowy background, how his mother had been an

American, that she had been born of a line of slave owners and a public whipmaster in the West Indies, even that – yes – his own mother was an infamous whore.

Rising from the table, Juan Carlos gallantly bowed to Lieutenant Balfour and said, 'Let me thank you for your hospitality. Let our future be one of friendship.'

Then, forcing himself to be charming, Juan Carlos added, 'Now please tell me exactly where I can find this bordello. I promise to watch myself.'

'Watch yourself?' Balfour regained his earlier mirth, saying, 'You will be watching the erotic shows which the fraudulent noblewoman stages on the top floor.'

Juan Carlos felt his face tighten; he forced himself to remain calm, inquiring, 'Erotic shows? I do not understand.'

'Pageants of passion. Displays of perversion. A theatre of sin and depravity the likes of which history has probably not seen since the decline of ancient Rome.'

'In New Orleans? On Rampart Street?'

'Yes, Conde Veradaga. Only three blocks from this very spot. The pleasure can be yours in a matter of few minutes. But, do take my advice. Guard the gold in your pocket. The Condesa Veradaga steals more than family names from young men.'

Juan Carlos could no longer control his anger; he nodded his farewell and turned away from the table, his mind racing with questions about what he might next find at – what was it called? Petit Jour?

*　　*　　*

Juanito easily located the bordello on Rampart Street, flourished a golden eagle, announced that he wished to visit the upstairs theatre and, then, ignoring the Yankee soldiers laughing, gambling, dancing with scantily attired prostitutes, he walked quickly up the moquette-covered steps to the top of the house.

A few men were already gathered on chaise longues encircling the small stage area; Juanito ordered a bottle of champagne from a waiter in a white jacket but did not drink it as he waited for the show; he lay brooding on the chaise longue about the incidents which had led him to this house, to New Orleans.

The events had been quick, unexpected, a succession of puzzling steps; a bootmaker in Havana told Juanito how he had just finished cobbling a pair of fine riding boots for a Mexican diplomat; the Mexican diplomat approached Juanito outside the shop, inviting him for a stroll, asking him if he knew anyone with a ship free to sail contraband weapons to the Confederate states; a carriage stopped alongside Juanito and the Mexican in the Plaza des Armas; an old man with piercing blue eyes acknowledged the Mexican and, fixing a cold stare on Juanito, said, 'Do not let Senor Calleja make too much of a profit off you, young man. The profit must be yours! As well as the adventure. You are young. Go, enjoy adventures. I would do such things myself if I were young like you. But I will never again leave Havana. The world comes to me.' The carriage rumbled away and, the last thing which Juanito had seen was a black woman peering out of the carriage's back window, the same black woman with the face scarred with burns. He asked, 'Who was that man? He was English, si? And that black woman with him! She haunts me!' The Mexican merely replied, 'Friends. Old and very powerful friends. He is Senor Richard Abdee and she is his lover.'

Then Juanito's nightmarish reminiscences about Havana were disturbed by young ladies emerging from beyond the stage to snuff the candles on the top floor at the bordello on Rampart Street; the show was beginning . . .

Two woodsmen returned home from a hunt; both men were white, wearing no clothing except for wide-brimmed mountain hats, their masculinity swinging large, limp, uncovered, between their hard-muscled thighs as they ambled nonchalantly onto the candle-lit stage; a pole rested on their broad shoulders and a naked girl, her ankles and feet tied to the pole with leather thongs, hung from the pole like a deer. The two men carried her towards the centre of the stage on the top floor of the bordello, Petit Jour.

A red-haired prostitute, dressed in a scant red gingham apron, rushed toward the two returning huntsmen, kissing the first man as if he were her husband, then bending to inspect what trophy he and his friend had brought home from the forest.

The two huntsmen dropped the pole onto the floor; the audience of Yankee officers groaned as the girl's body fell with a thud; the prostitute in the gingham apron began to examine the captive girl, turning her over, inspecting her thighs, arms, breasts; the hunters moved to unknot the naked girl from the pole but the 'wife' stopped them. She wanted the female trophy to remain in bondage.

The 'wife' continued her inspection of the trussed girl; she now sniffed at her smooth skin, pinching her here and there, then finally bent forward to inspect the furry patch between her bare legs; she spread open the girl's thighs and began tonguing her vagina.

One of the huntsmen nodded for his companion also to look at the two women; he began working his phallus with one fist as he approached the kneeling prostitute; he fell to his knees behind her and, without warning, roughly rammed his erect phallus into her anus.

The 'wife' jumped, miming surprise; her 'husband' pulled back his hand and a loud slap echoed through the theatre as he slapped his 'wife' sharply on her tender pink buttocks; he next pushed her head back down to the other female's vagina.

The second huntsman, his phallus now also standing erect from his mid-section, moved to kneel at one end of the pole to which the first girl was trussed. He began greasing the end of the pole from a pot on the floor; he kept his friend's 'wife' tonguing the other woman's vagina; he then nodded for his male companion to force the trussed female to perform the same act on his 'wife' and, soon, the two women greedily worked to satisfy one another with their darting tongues.

Both vaginas soon slippery with saliva, glistened like budding pink roses in the candle-light; the two huntsmen gripped their blood-hard phalluses; they untied the first female from the pole with a few deft pulls of the cords; she rolled onto her back as the 'wife' followed the same action.

Both ends of the pole, both greased from the pot, soon served as pleasure knobs for the two women; they stood at either end of the pole working their vaginal lips around the greased knobs; the two huntsmen stood between them, back to back, straddling the pole, making the women bend forward to take their phalluses in their mouths as they continued to fornicate themselves on the knobs of the pole.

*   *   *

Juanito left the theatre when one huntsman reached behind himself to finger his friend's hairy anus; Juanito did not want to know, to see what depravity would follow in this pleasure supplied by a woman who also called herself Veradaga. But was she his mother? Juanito ran down the steps, fighting the answer, '. . . yes . . yes . . . yes.'

*   *   *

From dawn until noon-time the fighting was light at Utoy Creek, Georgia; the Confederate troops were led by General Hood, Commanding Officer of Tennessee, who had also assumed command of the Louisiana regiments following Stonewall Jackson's death; the battle continued throughout the afternoon but with little more than periodic uproars of Federal cannons; the Confederate troops responded calmly to the steady report from the Yankee guns; David Abdee concentrated on the fine discipline of the men under his command; he was more proud of the valour shown by farm boys than the strategic genius of his superior officers.

The sky darkened into night early over Utoy Creek and, during the supper hour, shells began to sound loud above the tents of the Confederate encampment; the cannon roar grew louder and, as the officers rushed to their trenches, the sky glittered with air shells, a series of flashes which looked like bursting stars, a sky full of exploding stars which trailed puffs of luminescent white vapour.

Bullets cut faster through the air; the smell of gunpowder was pungent; the Confederates doubled their defence line returning the intense shooting; Federal bullets came faster, whistling across a low valley, breaking the ranks of General Hood's Louisiana supplement spread over a bald mound beyond the creek.

Again, the sky glittered with air artillery. David Abdee – his face covered with slime, his blue eyes glow-ing from the earthen mask – momentarily gazed at the exploding sky, the bright flashes, the smears of white smoke, mesmerized by its fleeting beauty; he did not think of the spectacle as war, but a momentary array he wanted to share – David thought, 'Tim! Oh, if Tim could see this sky! Tim, of all men would enjoy seeing this, I know it!'

David Abdee had thought increasingly of Tim in recent months during his campaigns through Georgia and Tennessee and, now, as bullets chuck, chuck, chucked faster around him, David again thought about the black boy with whom he had shared his childhood on Greenleaf Plantation, the man to whom he had personally entrusted Dragonard Hill.

Before the fatal shell struck David Abdee, he was aware he was going to die; he said, 'Lord, make Ham, Maybelle and Tim free . . . Give them land and a home and families, all the happiness of earth . . .'

David Abdee, not praying for himself, fell to his death at Utoy Creek, Georgia; a report of cannon fire struck his slim body, destroying him beyond any trace of identity, leaving no proof that he had been killed at Utoy Creek, Georgia, defending a cause to which he had been born, but in which he had never believed. He left only a wish.

Book Three

THE FUTURE

Chapter Fifteen

WILLS AND TESTAMENTS

Peter Abdee carefully weighed the reasons for going to New Orleans and try to locate Chloe. He spent the grey winter months of 1863 deciding whether or not he was foolish to continue torturing himself in loneliness, if there was any reason to be separated from Chloe and, deciding that he had suffered enough, he put his plans into motion to leave Dragonard Hill. Peter immediately felt a surge of excitement and energy, a welcome rebirth of cheerfulness in the anticipation of being reunited at long last with Chloe, an uplifting of mood which co-incided with the arrival of spring time.

There were many chores to perform both at Dragonard Hill and Greenleaf before departing for New Orleans. Peter was pleased with the cabins already built in the back hills; he saw that store-houses brimmed with ample food for his people, that provisions had been carefully buried in the ground, secreted in barns, stashed in the surrounding forests in the event that Federal – or even Confederate – soldiers should come through the neigh-bourhood on forays for food to supplement the army's dwindling supplies. Spring gardens were being planted and blossoms forecasted a heavy fruit crop. But even if a militia of nameless soldiers seized the bounty of both plantations, Peter knew that his people would not starve.

Apart from nutritional needs, Peter Abdee had also made specific legal instructions about what should happen to his slaves in the event of his death, that they would become the immediate property of his son, David; he also made a provision that if David Abdee were killed in the line of military duty, the slaves of Greenleaf and Dragonard immediately became the property of his daughter, Veronica. He could not include her husband, Royal, in this stipulation, as he could not foresee what future laws of heredity would be concerning black people.

But Peter included a clause in his testament which did consider future changes; he wrote an article which declared that, in the event of a Federal victory granting emancipation to all enslaved Negroes, the black people of Dragonard Hill and Greenleaf were to become title holders of small plots of ground which would be separate from the plantation, land already surveyed and houses being built on it; the Negroes could tend their own gardens as well as toil in the fields; they would share both the plantation work and the profits from its yield.

The peacefulness and quiet of Peter Abdee's last few days at Dragonard Hill were broken only by Posey's nervous visits from the kitchen annex to the main house.

Posey inundated Peter with anxious questions, asking, 'What if Master David returns when you be away, Master Peter?'

'David's a grown man. He can cope quite well by himself. He will eventually be master here some day. It will be good preparation.' Peter sat at his desk in the study, carefully filing the copies of his legal provisions to leave in the strong-box; he had told no one about the arrangements he had prepared; he had only briefly discussed them with David before his departure for the war; the recent lack of correspondence from David told Peter that it was wise to expedite the arrangements; Peter had long ago prepared himself for his son's death, although no word had come concerning that, either. Only silence.

'How long you plan to be gone, Master Peter? You

be too sickly to stay away from home for too long, Master Peter.'

Posey's questions and interference were uncharacteristic of his normally quiet composure in the presence of white people.

'I have no plans. I might not even be allowed to take the public road to New Orleans. There could well be military blockades stopping all civilian travel. I might have to turn around and come straight back home.'

'What if you gets to New Orleans and don't find Miss Chloe? Or what if she's married, Master Peter? What if Miss Chloe thinks you've forgotten her and married another man in the past two years?'

Posey's questions, both impertinent and troublesome, surprised Peter. But he patiently answered, 'If Miss Chloe is married, then I will give her and her husband my best regards, won't I? And I trust you'd also want me to extend your best wishes to her and whoever the . . . husband might be.'

'Oh, Master Peter!' Posey wailed. 'What if Yankees come here and try to rape me? Who's here to protect me? There'll be nobody in the house to watch after me!'

'I told you, Posey, the house will be locked. You shall sleep in the kitchen annex where you've been sleeping for the last twenty-five years. You are strong, Posey. No, I am not worried about you.'

'What about Miss Veronica? What if Miss Veronica writes a letter? What if a letter finally comes from Miss Veronica?'

'We also discussed that, Posey.' His patience fraying, Peter nevertheless continued, 'I told you that there's little chance of a letter coming from Veronica through the enemy lines. You are not to worry about that.'

'And Miss Vicky, Master Peter?' Posey persisted. 'What if you see Miss Vicky in New Orleans?'

Posey had never mentioned Vicky's name to Peter Abdee in twenty years. He answered, 'We do not know if Miss Vicky is in New Orleans or Havana, do we? Nor do we care.'

'Then what about them white trash patrollers? What if patrollers come here? What if they come here and cause trouble? Set the house afire? Chase the field niggers? Steal our chickens? Tie women and children and . . . me to the front pillars?'

Peter knew that Posey remembered a past siege of Dragonard Hill. He sternly replied, 'Posey, your mind is running away with itself. Every able bodied white man is away at war. I also told you that Maybelle's son, Tim, is coming here to live in the stable while I'm away. Tim is brave. He will watch over things. You just stay close to the kitchen and if anything should happen – '

Peter paused; he did not enjoy drawing attention to Posey's dubious sexuality; he lowered his head, speaking as he tied his second set of documents into a pouch to put into his saddle bag. 'You just remember what I told you, Posey. You just remember you have Veronica's children living in the North. You say you are related to Royal Selby in Boston.'

'Say I'm their granny,' Posey blurted. 'Will them Yankees believe that? That I'm a granny?'

Glancing at Posey's feminine attire, his androgynous features, Peter answered, 'Yes, Posey. They will believe it.'

He looked toward an open drawer on the desk, saying, 'There are manumission papers here, Posey. Documents which, when signed, will free slaves. Burn them if the Confederates come to the house. They will only anger the Confederates. If you see them coming, burn those papers and drape yourself in the Confederate flag. But you are clever. I do not have to worry about you, Posey. You are probably the strongest person on Dragonard Hill.'

Peter then rose from the desk feeling no regret, no remorse about leaving Dragonard Hill, the land to which he had been brought as a slave boy many years ago when it had been called 'The Star'. He felt as if he had done everything in his power for this land, its people, his family. The feeling was one of satisfaction, quiet satisfaction.

*   *   *

Maybelle stood between Ham and Tim in front of the main house at Greenleaf, facing Peter Abdee seated upon his horse; Maybelle waved goodbye, calling, 'You be careful on those bayou roads, Master Peter. The Yankees ain't the only enemies about.'

Neither she, Tim, nor Ham — who also now knew about Tim's secret cache of guns — had told their master about the patroller, Billy Cramer, receiving a confidential telegram from Montgomery, Alabama, that Tim had overheard the patrollers discussing a plan to incarcerate the black people of Greenleaf and Dragonard Hill to prevent them escaping to the North, that rumours had risen in the neighbourhood again about the Abdees being Abolitionists.

Ham squeezed Maybelle's waist, saying, 'Nobody knows this country better than Master Peter.'

Peter was anxious to leave; he danced his horse in front of the house, calling, 'I want you to keep an eye on things for me, Ham. And, Maybelle, you help Posey when it's needed.'

'Don't you worry about nothing,' Maybelle called. 'You just make sure you come back to us. And bring Miss Chloe home, too. Tell her we're needing her.'

'What do we do if trouble breaks out, Master Peter?'

Tim called, not wanting to raise Peter's suspicions by showing no sign of control, to betray that he and his family were plotting their own protection against troublesome white neighbours.

'You've got to see what kind of trouble it is. I'm sure there won't be anything you can't deal with, Tim. That is if it isn't the Yankee army. You have no choice with them. You can't fight an army which is defeating the entire South.'

Ham said, 'There won't be no trouble here, Master Peter. Nothing but a lot of hard work. The place will be looking the same when you gets back.'

Peter turned the horse and, heading toward the poplars lining the driveway, he called, 'I thank you again, Ham ... Maybelle ... Tim ...'

Maybelle stood between her husband and son; she stared blankly as Peter Abdee disappeared through the trees. Finally she broke the silence, saying, 'I'd like to "take care" of Miss Posey all right!'

'Now, honey, don't you have no cat fights!' Ham hugged his corpulent wife closer toward him.

'Cat fight! Hell, Posey ain't even got no ... pussy!'

'Ma!' Tim grinned at his mother.

'Boy,' Maybelle said, turning to him, 'you got work to do. And you be careful on that road, too. Who you taking with you in that wagon to Dragonard Hill?'

'Bullshot.'

Ham advised, 'You just waits a few minutes for Master Peter to get a good head start on you. He might ask you why for you taking hay from here to Dragonard Hill.'

Maybelle glanced one more time at the poplars, asking, 'Do you think he'll ever come back here?'

'Who?'

'Master Peter.'

'Why you say that, woman?'

178

'He just seems too happy to be leaving.' Maybelle shook her head and, walking toward the front door, she mumbled, 'Tim, you do like your Pa says. You be careful in that wagon, you hear?'

'Ma, why you acting like the cat that sneaked the cream?' Tim asked.

'What you mean, boy?' Maybelle flared. 'You say I'm acting sneaky? I'm proud of hiding things? Well, let me tell you, I ain't proud. But I knows there's nothing Master Peter can do. He's been fighting lies and ugliness all his life. He's seen more than his share of suffering and disappointments and hardships. Did you notice how much better he looked today? Almost like some boy going out courting his sweetheart. Do you think I'd ruin that? No, boy. I think it's time us niggers start fighting for ourselves. We've been hiding behind Master Peter for too long. So, you hop to it, boy! You've be man enough to lay your hands on some guns, we better all be able to use them.'

She nodded and disappeared into the house.

'She's a good woman,' Ham said.

'Yep. You be a lucky man, Pa.'

'Your time will come, son. Don't give up no hope. The Lord's got a nice gal tucked away for you some place.'

* * *

Bullshot, Tim's trustworthy friend from the slave-quarters at Greenleaf, sat alongside him in the wagon and called over the rumble of wooden wheels slowly progressing down the public road toward Dragonard Hill. 'Master Peter get off for New Orleans?'

'Just after breakfast.'

'Reckon the trip's got to do with Alphonse St Cloude?'

'Nobody's heard a word of Alphonse for over three

years,' Tim called, the leather reins slack in his hands. 'Master Peter's gone to talk to Miss Chloe. I reckon he'll bring her back home.'

'You tell him about the patrollers planning to raid both plantations and pen up us niggers? Or you lets your Ma and Pa tell him about that?'

'Nobody told him,' Tim replied. 'No use to worry him. Nothing he can do.'

Bullshot looked at Tim, saying, 'You've starting to feel some loyalty to him, ain't you? More than you used to.'

'We're like his family, I guess.'

Bullshot could not argue the fact; he answered, 'Master Peter, he's been good to us all. Been good building us those new cabins. Like us having our own private little town.'

'That's one more reason for those folks in Troy to hate us,' Tim said, lazily lowering his eyes against the warm sun, his body jostling in rhythm with the plodding wagon. 'We don't need them. We got all we needs for everybody between Greenleaf and Dragonard Hill.'

Pausing, Tim said, with no apparent concern, 'I wonder when they attack if it'll be on two fronts?'

'You mean Greenleaf and Dragonard Hill?'

Tim nodded. 'What niggers they'll go for first?'

Bullshot pondered the question. 'Probably Dragonard Hill. It's bigger. More important to Master Peter.'

'That's what we was thinking. Pa and me. Glad to hear you thinking the same. That's why you and me be taking this load of hay to Dragonard Hill.'

'They gots all the hay they need over there. Gots more hay than us.'

'Not this kind. Feel it.'

Bullshot turned on the wooden seat and, sticking a hand into the hay piled onto the wagon bed, he felt the butt of a musket.

He smiled. 'How many?'

'Three dozen.'

'Ammunition?'

'More than half.'

'We hide them all in one place?'

'No. Different spots around the big house.'

'That going to take long?'

Tim looked at his friend. 'Why you ask that?'

'I wants to get back tonight and see Hettie.'

'Hettie? You still poking that wench?'

'I likes Hettie!'

'She's trouble,' Tim worked his jaw, finally asking, 'You never told Hettie nothing about these guns?'

Bullshot ignored the question.

Tim repeated, 'You ain't never told Hettie nothing about these guns?'

'She's black! She's on our side!'

'You told her!' Tim shouted, his fists gripping the reins.

Bullshot shrugged. 'Never said I did.'

'Well, you better not. You better not tell that Hettie wench nothing. She's nothing but what they call a "power poker".'

'A what?'

'You ask Hettie when you see her tonight. You ask your Hettie what she be.'

*　　*　　*

Billy Cramer used a stick to draw the plan of attack in the dirt yard in front of Troy's general store; he kicked at a yellow she-dog, her moulting belly lined with teats, to secure a wider expanse on the ground to illustrate his lecture to the other patrollers grouped around him.

'Toke Benedict, Fred Biler, Dutch Duggan, the boys

from Carterville and thereabouts will meet us here on the west road,' Cramer said, making an x in the dirt with his stick.

'That be just east of the Dragonard boneyard,' said Burt Thomas.

'Whites folks call them cemeteries,' Cramer mumbled to his ancient enemy and then continued with the plan he had been carefully devising with the patrollers in Carterville during the past months.

'There's the old Grouse place . . . here,' Cramer made another mark in the dirt. 'Nobody's lived there since old Claudia Grouse got hacked to death years ago near the crossroads.'

'Never did solve that mystery, did they?' Thomas interrupted.

Cramer shot the silver-toothed old man an irritable glance and proceeded, 'The first niggers we take will be penned up at the Grouse place. The pens are already made.'

Thomas said to the man next to him, 'Going to need a few hundred acres of pens to prisonate all them Abdee slaves.'

Cramer chose to reply to Thomas's point by speaking to the entire group. He explained, 'After we make the first raids on Dragonard, the coons there will start shitting themselves. We then take command of the hill –'

' "Hill"?' It was Thomas speaking again. 'What hill?'

Throwing down his stick with anger, Cramer cursed, 'God damn it, you going to let me speak to these men or ain't you?'

'Go ahead. Speak.'

Anger and frustration consumed Billy Cramer. His face reddened as he announced, 'Another telegram just came from Montgomery today. Another telegram telling that some one special is coming all the way here to ride with us.'

'Special? How special? Who's coming here from the capital?'

Cramer did not reply to the question. He knew that Thomas would abuse, perhaps even laugh at him, if he confided that Peter Abdee's illegitimate son – the octoroon dandy, Alphonse St Cloude – was riding from Montgomery to help the patrollers attack Dragonard Hill.

He stuck both hands in his pockets and, moving toward the store's porch, he said, 'Until some certain unnamed parties stop disturbing us, let's go over what guns, whips, billy-clubs and dynamite we got to use if we need it.'

*   *   *

Bullshot lay in the darkness of the tackroom at Greenleaf Plantation with Maybelle's kitchen helper, Hettie; the air reeked from leather saddles and harnessing hanging from the rafters and walls; Bullshot's stocky body pumped ferociously between Hettie's spread legs and he asked, 'What is you, Hettie?'

'What's you wants me to be?'

'What's a power poker, Hettie?' Bullshot whispered, remembering what Tim had told him about Hettie this morning on the drive to Dragonard Hill. 'I hears that's what you be? Some kind of . . . power poker.'

The question surprised Hettie; she did not remember using the brazen term lately to describe herself, her ambitions, her ulterior motives for making love; she asked, 'Who put those words in your brain, nigger?'

'Nobody particular.'

'Tim? He told you them words?'

Bullshot tried to continue his phallic stride, maintaining

the build to sexual orgasm as he said, 'Why you ask Tim?'

Hettie wondered if Tim might at last be interested in her; she knew he was the last desirable person of authority left at Greenleaf on Dragonard Hill; she also knew that Bullshot was not clever and she said, to test him, 'Tim couldn't have told you them words, Bullshot. Tim's gone to stay at Dragonard Hill.'

'How you know that?' Bullshot moved more slowly.

'I see you go both riding together this morning through the poplars in the hay wagon. But I sees just you come back to Greenleaf, alone.'

Bullshot suspected more than ever that Hettie desired Tim and he felt jealousy for the first time; he asked, 'You sorry Tim don't come back? That he's stayed at Dragonard Hill?'

Hettie, wrapping her arms around Bullshot's thick neck, whispered into his ear, 'I'm glad *you* comes back. I'm glad, Bullshot, you be here with me because . . .'

Hettie still feared that a man's seed would become planted in her womb; she kissed Bullshot's ear but, knowing he was reaching his climax, she slid down quickly beneath his body, disengaging his penis from her vagina, groping it in her hand as she began to lick, mouth, praise his large sac of testicles. She did not want to carry Bullshot's − nor any other field nigger's − baby inside her belly for nine long months.

Chapter Sixteen

A PROPOSAL

The small clapboard house, with flower boxes decorating the front windows, was one of the many similar cottages dotting the ramparts in the vicinity of Faubourg Maurigny in New Orleans; they had been built for free women of colour who lived secluded lives as the discreet mistresses of white gentlemen.

Peter Abdee thought about the tradition of white men 'keeping' their coloured mistresses in these cottages, how they met the young girls at the gala octoroon balls on Orleans streets, how the girls were reared and educated solely to be lovers of white men; he knew that Chloe had been born from such a union and raised by her 'Tante Marie' to continue in this tradition practised only in New Orleans.

The sight of the Federal 'stars and stripes' flag fluttering over the U.S. Mint Building at the foot of Esplanade Ridge gave Peter a momentary jolt; he then realized that, regardless of what government occupied the city, many traditions would never give way in New Orleans, that its citizens were stubborn, arrogant, proud of their heritage.

The tradition of octoroon mistresses was one of the most misunderstood practices in New Orleans. Strangers to the city frequently believed the female gens de couleur libre were prostitutes but, in reality, the young women were raised and guarded with as much care as a daughter born of proper Creole parentage.

Octoroon women had golden coloured skin, sparkling dark eyes, pure white teeth and curvaceous figures which tempted any man. But white men seldom escorted their coloured mistresses in public and, consequently, the exotic females befriended one another and were seen in groups at the opera, often groomed more meticulously, dressed more opulently, than the wives of the men who kept them.

Peter Abdee tied his weary horse to the post in front of Chloe's small cottage; the day-long ride had been hard and although he planned to stay as usual in the St Charles Hotel to protect Chloe's reputation in the strict octoroon community, he had to discover her whereabouts as soon as possible.

Opening the wooden gate, Peter saw that the paint was peeling on the small house but that the front yard was well-maintained, the porch neatly swept and the windows sparkling clean. He knew that someone was definitely living in the house.

Peter gently rapped on the door's pane of frosted glass and, waiting for a reply, he felt a growing anticipation, a warm inner glow as he stood on the porch, almost the youthful excitement of a suitor.

He again knocked on the pane of glass, now wondering where he would look for Chloe if she was not here; he suddenly heard a bolt slide inside the door, the door opened and he stood facing a small woman whom he did not immediately recognize: her face was devoid of all cosmetics, her black hair knotted at the nape of her neck, her clothing – faded, patched, but clean.

Peter was unable to speak; he could not believe this small frail woman was . . . Chloe.

But neither did Chloe speak; she stared up at Peter, her eyes widening with shock.

'May I come in?' Peter finally asked.

'Monsieur?' she gasped.

Peter smiled; he recognized the voice, the politeness he had forgotten; he stepped forward and wrapping the small woman in his arms, he whispered, 'My love.'

Chloe, gripping Peter around the waist, buried her face in his chest and began to sob, 'You should not have done this, monsieur. You should not have come.'

Peter ignored Chloe's weak protests; he stood stroking the back of her head, knowing that he had indeed made the correct decision to leave Dragonard Hill.

*   *   *

Chloe awkwardly insisted that Peter come into the cottage; Peter beat the dust from his clothes, shut the door behind him and, ignoring the front parlour's furnishings, he announced, 'I've come to take you home.'

Chloe, fidgeting nervously with her hands, answered, 'I have never argued with you, but – '

'Why did you run away, Chloe? Why did you not answer my letters?'

'You do not realize how much I do love you . . .'

'Love!' Peter stepped forward, putting his hand on her shoulder. 'Love is important, yes. But so is sharing love. To be together.'

Chloe kept her head lowered, saying, 'Pride is important, too, monsieur.'

'Pride? Or do you mean self-respect, Chloe? Or is it the lack of self-respect? What you wrongly interpret as shame.'

Peter lifted Chloe's chin with his hand, explaining, 'I suspected in the last few months why you did not come back to Dragonard Hill. Your reasons revolved around Alphonse, didn't they? I do not know your exact reasons, but here is something else for you to consider.'

Peter spoke honestly, 'I have sired five children, Chloe. Three daughters. Two sons. One son with you, Alphonse. But Alphonse is your first, your only child. So I know a few things you don't know. I know that the important person in my life is me!' He thumbed his chest, continuing, 'Me and the person I love. And I love you, Chloe. I truly love you.'

'And I love – ' she stopped, closed her eyes, trying not to weep.

'Here, come close to me,' Peter whispered, enveloping Chloe in his arms. 'Come close to me, stay close to me.'

Chloe could no longer hold back her tears; she fell against Peter's chest and he immediately swept her light body from the floor in his arms; he carried her to the bedroom he saw beyond the door opening from the parlour and, soon, they lay side by side on a divan; Peter began to cover Chloe's tear-stained face with kisses, assuring her that she need never again have any fears, that they would never again be separated; he then kissed her hands, and, seeing the callouses, he chastised her for working too hard; Peter finally lowered his mouth to Chloe's lips; he tasted the familiar sweetness and began to reassure her, too, of their physical love.

Peter had always enjoyed love-making with Chloe but the act had never been so meaningful, so sacred as it was this evening in the small cottage near the ramparts; Chloe and Peter did not speak as they lay naked on the divan except to whisper one another's names, to exchange assurances of devotion. Chloe finally began to scream ecstatically as they clung to one another in the peak of their physical nearness.

The weeks, months, years of separation disappeared as Chloe and Peter lay fulfilled in one another's arms. Chloe gently touched Peter's sunburned neck, whispered,

'You have neglected yourself, monsieur. No one has been trimming your hair.'

Peter smiled, again brushing his lips against Chloe's cheek. 'Neglect? What about you? We must go shopping for you, my love. Your wardrobe is threadbare.'

'The city has changed,' Chloe quickly answered. 'There is little to purchase in the shops. And, what is available is so exorbitantly expensive. Why, the only women who have new fabrics for dresses, new bonnets, new leather shoes are women who befriend the Northern soldiers, shameless women who . . .'

She suddenly stopped.

Peter knowingly said, 'You've seen Vicky?'

Chloe's eventual reply was soft, not damning, 'Yes. She prospers.'

'She still runs that . . . house?' This was the first time he had spoken about his daughter's shameless occupation.

'Northern soldiers are billeted there. Perhaps she has no choice. We all must survive in our own way.'

Peter could not stifle a smile. He said, 'Thank the Lord that Goths have not sacked New Orleans! My own daughter would be swathed in bearskins and drinking blood from a horn flagon!'

Pulling Chloe tightly against him, Peter said, 'Oh, I am so happy I've found you. That's what's important to me.'

Chloe asked, 'You will be staying at the St Charles Hotel?'

'Yes,' he replied. 'I have always respected your reputation. I know how strictly your aunt raised you. I know how her old friends wag their tongues. I will stay at the St Charles until you assure me that you will come home to Dragonard Hill.' He kissed Chloe on both eyes, adding, 'Come home – as my bride.'

'Monsieur,' Chloe gasped, 'that's a proposal!'

189

Peter nodded. 'Men become stupid with age. But not me. I have finally become wise. I am asking you to marry me. I know it is a monumental step. I know there is the question of blood. So do not rush your decision. But I will not go back to Dragonard Hill until I have an answer. I pledge that. I have never been fond of New Orleans. I have always been too much of a bumpkin. But I will not leave here until you tell me whether or not you'll become . . . Mrs Abdee.'

Chloe did not look at Peter as she confessed, 'I do not know if I can ever go back to Dragonard Hill. That is unfair to you, I know, but . . .'

Peter smiled. 'Then we can go someplace else. I've learned it is not the land that is important. The important thing is – ' he squeezed her small hand, ' – you. Please consider it. My proposal is serious.'

Chapter Seventeen

OLD GHOSTS

Vicky appreciated General Turkel's presence in the house on Rampart Street; William Turkel was a tall man, with a commanding presence, and he gave Vicky a sense of added security in a city occupied by the enemy.

Both Turkel and Vicky shared a mutual distance from politics; they similarly viewed the Civil War and occupation of New Orleans as no more than an economic disagreement between the Northern and Southern states rather than a high moral struggle touted by politicians, clergymen, journalists.

William Turkel, tall, with black hair touched with silver at the temple, was a sexually robust man who enjoyed more than a normal interest in love-making. He and Vicky both viewed sex objectively, often even having a prostitute and a soldier perform privately for them in Vicky's bedroom when they themselves were too fatigued to participate in the sexual act but, nevertheless, desired to watch, to feel, to make lewd comments, to laugh, to be diverted in an otherwise bleak city.

'Why do you stay in this damp city?' Turkel also repeatedly asked Vicky. He did not enjoy New Orleans.

'I'm a business woman,' she replied, 'and until I find a better economic proposition in another city, then I remain in New Orleans.'

Turkel first began jokingly suggesting to Vicky that, at the conclusion of the war, he would not return to his wife in Philadelphia, but that he and Vicky would travel west together and live in San Francisco as decadent, hedonistic lovers.

He extolled, 'Until you've been to California, you haven't enjoyed life. The city of San Francisco holds all the delights of the Orient as well as offering hostelries equal to any in New Orleans, up north in Boston, New York, Philadelphia, probably even Europe.'

Vicky did not immediately respond to the lure of the west. But Turkel's repeated suggestions that they escape there together gave her reason to consider the future, to evaluate her contentment as a bordello's mistress.

Also Vicky saw that Turkel appreciated her more than a woman with a sexual stable, a female entrepreneur of exotic fantasies, but as a woman who ate, drank, enjoyed travel as much as any other person. In brief, that she was somebody with whom he could happily live out his life.

Vicky consequently began to confide in Turkel about her past, how she had been born Victoria Abdee in northern Louisiana, how she had gone to school in Boston where she had met her first husband, a Yankee fop named Duncan Webb who had come south with her and worked as a male whore in this very bordello in the days when it had been owned by a Negress from St Kitts named Naomi; Vicky also told Turkel how she had later married a crippled Cuban aristocrat called Juan Carlos Veradaga who had banned her from returning to Havana. She even confided in Turkel that the Negress, Naomi, had gone to Havana and given her possession of this bordello. Vicky knew that Turkel enjoyed – believed – the complexities of Fate and she confided how Naomi and her own grand-father – a man named Richard Abdee – had once been lovers on the Caribbean island of St Kitts, that her grand-father had long ago been the public whipmaster there, a mercenary post instituted by the British government and called the 'dragonard'.

General Turkel, his blue eyes twinkling mischievously, entered Vicky's office late one spring afternoon and airily announced, 'I think it might interest you, Condesa, that there is a man named Abdee staying at the St Charles Hotel.'

Vicky raised her eyes from the ledger on which she was working. 'Abdee?'

'Peter Abdee,' Turkel said, as he sat down in the wing chair across from Vicky's desk and unfastened the gilt and silver sabre from his sash. 'Dragonard Hill Plantation.'

'That's my . . . father!'

He nodded. 'I remember.'

'Did you speak to him?'

'Speak to him? Why? To ask for your hand in marriage? I can hardly do that, my dear. I still have a wife!'

'Stop teasing me!' Vicky threw down her pen and demanded, 'How do you know this?'

'How do I know every frivolous fact in New Orleans? My spies tell me. They tell me every detail that is not vital. I know every newcomer's name in this city. Every farmer who comes to town with a squash. Every darkie wearing a pair of green shoes. But do I ever hear about foreigners? Gun-runners? Spies? Oh, no! I hear nothing important!'

Vicky now ignored him; she sat back in her chair, considering the fact that her father was staying only a few blocks away from her; she wondered if he had at last come to New Orleans to find Chloe. Or, was he here for some other reason? Because of Alphonse? Or David? She had completely lost touch with everybody, did not know who was dead, who was alive, who was friend or foe.

Closing her leather-bound ledger, Vicky sprang from her chair and said, 'I have not been outside this dump for – what? One year? Two years? That's ridiculous! Absurd!'

'What about the roof last night? Or do you forget my manly charms so easily? Do you not call making love under the stars – '

'Stop it! I do not mean like that. I mean going into public! On the street! I have kept myself hidden inside here, knowing that the damned citizens would probably stone me in the streets!'

Turkel nodded in agreement. 'Probably rip off some of those fine clothes. I might even enjoy watching that.'

Standing in front of the cheval mirror in one corner of the office, Vicky appraised her hair, the mound of henna ringlets kept stylishly curled by her private hairdresser. She tilted her head to one side, saying, 'I think black would be appropriate. Black crepe de chine. A black shawl. An inconspicuous bonnet. But with a veil, of course. And maybe . . . pearls? Do you think pearls, William?'

Turkel stood behind Vicky and, playfully biting her neck, he said, 'If I can get you to walk four blocks, who knows my powers? I might even get you to cross the continent with me!'

Vicky, too excited at the prospect of finally stepping outside Petit Jour, too interested in her wardrobe, pushed away Turkel's mouth and gibed, 'Go play army!'

*   *   *

Vicky, surprised by the lack of attention she received along Rampart Street in her elegant black crepe de chine dress, walked quickly down the wooden banquette-lined street, with the same bow-fronted chemist, shops, cafés behind courtyards, jewellers and dressmakers which had been there when she had last ventured out into public. She noticed little difference in the occupied city, but not eager to study it now, she hurried toward the St Charles Hotel.

Passing through the marble columns fronting the neoclassical façade, Vicky majestically swept into the palm-filled lobby and walked directly to the clerk's desk. She demanded, 'Could you please tell me the number of the room Mr Abdee is in? Mister Peter Abdee, Dragonard Hill Plantation.'

'Your name, Madam?'

Vicky paused, considering whether she should give her maiden name or –

Tossing her head in the air, she said, 'Veradaga! Condesa Veradaga.'

'Condesa . . . Veradaga?'

'That is correct.' She prepared herself for the first insult. 'Is something wrong?'

The clerk's voice remained calm, even polite, as he replied, 'But I did not know the Count was travelling with his . . . is Madam the Count's wife?'

'Wife?' Vicky did not understand. 'What Count?'

'Count Juan Carlos Veradaga.'

Vicky suddenly felt her knees weaken; she immediately wondered if her husband had not died, if she had been told lies. Next, she considered the possibility of William Turkel playing a joke on her. The possibilities confused her. She remembered her original mission and asked, 'Peter Abdee? He is not registered here? Peter Abdee of Dragonard Hill?'

'Yes, Countess. Mr Abdee is also registered at the hotel. But Mr Abdee spends little time here. I shall most gladly send a boy to Mr Abdee's room to see if he is presently in the hotel . . .'

The clerk paused and looking beyond Vicky, he suddenly called, 'Count? Count Veradaga?'

Vicky grasped his hand whispering, 'No! Please!'

But it was too late.

'Si, Senor?' The voice was rich, youthful and came from alongside her.

'This lady – ' the hotel clerk began, ' – the Condesa Veradaga.'

Vicky slowly turned her head and saw a young man with golden brown skin, glossy black hair, a handsome youth dressed in immaculate linens, a fashionable stock tied around his aristocratic neck, a coat of fine wool.

She murmured, 'Juanito.'

'Juanito?' he repeated. The use of his family nickname confirmed his worst suspicions. He felt his fists clenching.

The image of the young man then blurred to Vicky; she felt herself becoming faint; she heard the clerk frantically call for assistance, 'The lady! The Countess! She is fainting!'

Vicky felt a strong arm support her, a voice saying, 'Por favor. Allow me.'

*　　　*　　　*

Vicky felt brandy reviving her strength; she focused on the dark-haired young man sitting alongside her on a red velvet settee positioned behind a drooping palm tree in one corner of the hotel's lobby.

He asked, 'Who is this Abdee man you ask to see?'

'Is that the first thing you have to say . . . Juanito?'

'What do you want me to ask? "How's business"? Are your guests comfortable?' Juanito then warned, 'Do not call me by the name used only by my family and dear friends. I have seen you. I have been to your . . . theatricals. I do not want a woman like you to call me fond names.'

'You know me?'

'All I want to know,' he paused, sarcastically adding, 'Condesa! I know all I want to know about you and your shameless masquerade.'

'The only masquerade I ever lived was my marriage to your father.'

Juanito flared, 'Do not speak ill of my father, woman!'

Vicky kept her voice low, answering, 'You are correct in speaking so to me: I was untrue. But not to your father. I was untrue to myself.'

'Is this life you lead here true? Are your scandals here befitting your true character . . . Condesa?'

'If you harbour as much hatred for me in your heart as you have in your voice, why do you waste your time talking to me? Leave! Get away from me! I do not have to suffer your insolence too! I suffered enough from the last Juan Carlos Veradaga!'

'I just want to confirm my suspicions. To see with my own eyes that my mother is a whore!'

'No, your mother is not a whore, you ungrateful wretch!' Vicky said, sitting forward on the velvet settee. 'Your mother merely lives off whores' money. But don't you be so pompous! Your sainted father grew rich from selling slaves to cruel Cuban planters! Damning Africans to work two, three years on a finca and then die! I'll hear no sermons from you, little Juan Carlos!'

Stopping, Vicky shook her head, saying, 'No, I am wrong to get angry with you. You were obviously raised not to know anything about your background. You grew up in a completely sheltered world. So, go back there. Leave this city. This country. Return to Havana. That damned Palacio Veradaga in Jesu Maria! Those boring banquets in that cold, heartless comedor! Those dreary rides round and round the Plaza des Armas. That ridiculous pomposity of the cardinals, the dowagers, the good families, their chaste daughters. Yes, I am certain you deserve all the boredom Havana has to offer young snobs like you. Do not waste your time in America. In . . .'

Stopping again, she asked, 'Why *are* you in America? This country is at war. So what are you doing here, Conde Juan Carlos Veradaga?'

Juanito rose abruptly from the velvet settee and, bowing stiffly, he said, 'Let us both forget about this meeting. I am returning to Havana. I hope never to see you again.' He turned, walked away, the heels of his high polished boots echoing across the tessellated marble floor.

The clerk approached Vicky, saying, 'I sent a boy upstairs, Madam, and Mister Abdee is not in his room today. Do you wish to leave a message?'

Vicky gathered the skirts of her black crepe de chine gown, answering, 'No thank you. I've had enough family for one day.'

She wanted nothing but to return to Petit Jour, never to emerge in the world. Except, perhaps, to go to San Francisco. This city was becoming too crowded with ghosts.

*   *   *

Juanito had previously arranged to meet the Confederate officer, Lieutenant Balfour, in a Baronne Street café this evening to bid him farewell; Juanito had learned that Cajun fishermen made regular trips down the Bayou St John at fixed hours and he planned to bribe these Canadian Frenchmen transplanted in Louisiana to row him to his ship anchored safely beyond the southernmost bayou.

Balfour was not waiting for Juanito when he arrived at the café still seething with anger from the accidental meeting with his mother; he fumed about the arrogant manner in which she had spoken about his father, the lack of shame she displayed to the world, her consorting with Yankee soldiers in New Orleans.

Ordering a glass of cool tea, Juanito momentarily wondered if Balfour's lateness was due to some trouble, if his true identity had been discovered by Federal troops, that the Northerners had learned that Balfour was not a frivolous man of fashion, but, in reality a Confederate spy who kept in close contact with General Beauregard's headquarters in Montgomery, Alabama.

Juanito began sipping his tea and soon remembered his own problems, the confirmation that his mother indeed was a shameless woman, the vile things she had said about his father building a fortune on the lives – and deaths – of African slaves.

Juanito had known his father's enterprises had included slave-dealing. But recalling how his mother had spoken so bitterly about slavery, he wondered if he himself had never seriously considered the implications of buying and selling human lives. Was he shallow as his mother had accused? Was he – like his father – a hypocrite?

'Who is she to talk about hypocrisy?' Juanito angrily asked himself and waved to the waiter to bring him a whisky. To hell with tea!

Juanito next remembered the old Englishman who had arranged for him to buy crates of Spanish-made rifles from a Mexican agent in Havana, a leather-faced old man who lived in Havana named Abdee – Richard Abdee.

Abdee. Juanito now remembered that he had heard the hotel desk clerk mention the same name – Abdee – to his mother. But he was certain that it could not be the same man; he clearly recalled how old Richard Abdee had said to him that he never again wanted to venture out into the world, that he was content to remain in Havana with his mistress.

Juanito sat in the café on Baronne Street, vividly recollecting his meeting with Richard Abdee and the Negress who wore a black veil to cover her burned face; Abdee had not allowed the Mexican agent to haggle with Juanito over the price of the Spanish firearms; the old Englishman had seemed to be intent on Juanito having a reason to venture from Havana, to sail the contraband guns to New Orleans.

Juanito racked his brains for more details of the brief meeting which had been so mysteriously arranged between himself and Richard Abdee in Havana's seamy district of Regla. He had suspected at the time that there were vital facts not being told to him, pieces of a puzzle to which he was not privy, as if the old Englishman might even be testing him, acquainting himself with him, trying his mettle.

'Damn it!' Juanito said aloud, feeling frustrated, manipulated, like a pawn in some sinister plot.

'Juan Carlos, you are so good to wait for me!'

Juanito turned and saw Balfour hurriedly approaching him.

Balfour, ordering a whisky for himself and another for Juanito, sank to a chair, confiding, 'I had to send a telegram to Montgomery. I was late because I had to invent a new code. I received word this morning that a crowd of old codgers up-country are attacking one of the South's most prosperous plantations. Peter Abdee is a fine man. He's not a friend of mine but I'd hate to see jealous men burn Dragonard Hill to the ground and haul off his slaves.'

'Abdee?' Juanito was certain now that he was in a dream.

'Yes, Peter Abdee. Do you know him?'

'No. But I heard the name only this afternoon. He is staying at my hotel.'

'Abdee? In New Orleans?' Balfour looked into the distance, musing, 'I wonder if Peter Abdee's come to town because he also has heard what a scandal his daughter has become?'

'Daughter?' Juanito felt a cold perspiration break out on his forehead.

Balfour nodded, 'Oh, yes. I didn't tell you. That's the maiden name of the bogus Condesa. The other Veradaga. She's one of Peter Abdee's daughters. Oh, he might be an honourable retiring planter who stays in the country, but his family – ' Balfour shook his head, ' – one daughter a whore. Her sister married a free slave. A son implicated in Abolitionist activities. Another son, a half-caste wastrel who has somehow inveigled his way into the Confederate Postal Service.'

Stopping, Balfour asked, 'My good friend? What have I said again to upset you? You've suddenly gone pale!'

Juanito raised one hand for Balfour to be silent, asking, 'You say men are preparing to attack the Abdee plantation? And this . . . Peter Abdee? He is a good man?'

'One of the soundest. The salt of our earth. His plantation is quite impressive. It's called Dragonard Hill. Peter Abdee is one of the few men in the South who has a humanitarian point of view regarding Negroes. It's a shame his family has grown into nothing but profligates and whores like the Condesa Veradaga – '

Juanito bolted up from his chair.

'Where are you going?' Balfour asked. 'Juan Carlos? Where are you going? What have I said now? Come back! I must tell you about the Cajun fishermen! The fishing boat waiting to take you past the delta!'

Juanito did not stop; he now had all the clues to the puzzle but if he were to emerge honourable, not be vindictive, he must pay one last call to his mother's house.

Chapter Eighteen

THE CONFEDERATE CAPTAIN

The sight of a fully-uniformed Confederate officer galloping into the sleepy town of Troy brought people to their windows and doorsteps; Alphonse St Cloude had stolen a Dixie grey captain's uniform and necessary documents to travel safely from Montgomery to Troy; he reined his horse to an abrupt halt in front of the general store; a cloud of thick yellow dust enveloped him as he hopped off the horse, quickly tied the reins to the post and rushed up the steps to greet the patrollers lounging on their chairs and on the splintery floor.

Alphonse doffed his officer's hat, bowed low to Billy Cramer and dutifully said, 'Captain St Cloude reporting to you, sir.'

Then, remembering the long established feud between Billy Cramer and Burt Thomas, Alphonse turned to Thomas and announced, 'General Beauregard sends his personal greetings to all the law-abiding citizens of Troy, Mr Thomas, sir.'

'Beauregard? General Beauregard sends hello to . . . me?' Thomas stared in amazement at Alphonse St Cloude; he was too impressed with the personal greeting to complain that Cramer's mysterious connection in Montgomery was Alphonse St Cloude, to remind the rest of the patrollers and other people gathering around the porch that Alphonse had Negro blood in his veins.

Resuming an impressive pose, Alphonse replied with military crispness, 'The General sends regards to you,

Mr Thomas, as well as to all the patrollers of Troy.'

Alphonse noticed out of the corner of his eye that Billy Cramer had suddenly relaxed, that he was pleased how Alphonse was ingratiating himself with Thomas and the other racially prejudiced patrollers.

Cramer, his thumbs hooked around his suspenders, bragged, 'We made all the preparations to start flushing out that Abolitionist nest, St Cloude.'

Alphonse was not surprised that Cramer ignored his title; he had not expected to be addressed as 'Captain'. He pompously replied, 'We are pleased, sir, with your thoroughness.'

Burt Thomas, stepping forward to study Alphonse's grey uniform, drawled, 'You know the place to be Dragonard Hill?'

'I know, sir.'

'That does not bother you, boy? Us riding on your Pappy?' Burt Thomas prided himself on his frankness.

'When the Confederacy is involved, how could I argue, sir? I suspect that the only problem will come from . . . Mr Abdee himself.'

'Abdee ain't home,' Thomas said, his head tilted to one side. 'Abdee's gone to New Orleans.'

Alphonse smiled. 'Then you gentlemen have both time and the law on your side.' He realized his own luck.

Thomas scratched the stubble on his chin, saying, 'You ain't a hundred per cent white, boy. But I do believe you've changed your ways since going to the Army. I do believe the Army's made a man out of you.'

'More than a man, sir,' Alphonse said, swelling his chest. 'A Captain!' Then, turning to face the other patrollers, he announced so that they, as well as the growing audience in the street, could hear, 'Too bad we can't claim the same for my step-brother, David Abdee. You know the Army has proof he's involved in Abolitionist activity. Working in collusion with his sister up north and certain slaves at Dragonard Hill.'

Billy Cramer, eager to regain the centre of attention, boasted, 'Don't worry no more about that. We're making our first raid tomorrow night. Got to protect the countryside.'

'That's a mistake,' grumbled Burt Thomas. 'I still think tonight's best. Tomorrow's too late.'

'Don't rush things, damn it!' Cramer boomed. 'The boys from Carterville ain't finding it easy to get weapons.'

'Gentlemen!' Alphonse pleaded. 'Please! We must all work in harmony!'

'The boy's right!' Cramer said, stepping alongside Alphonse. 'You ain't hog-raising now, Thomas. You be helping Beauregard's cause.'

Turning to Alphonse, Cramer said, 'Tell me one thing, boy. Tell me how the Army finally got the goods on them nigger-loving Abdees? Got the proof for us peace-lovers to finally shove their faces in the muck?'

'Letters,' Alphonse solemnly answered. 'Incriminating letters written from Dragonard Hill. The Abdees used their nigger cook as a front to pass information to the Abolitionist group up north.'

'Nigger cook?' Cramer gasped. 'But niggers ain't supposed to be reading or writing? That's against the law!'

Alphonse shrugged, 'Either way, I am ashamed to say that people close to me are law-breakers. Either way, by running slaves or breaking slave rules.'

Brushing the dirt from his clothes, Alphonse then said, 'Now I would like to rest, take some refreshment and listen more closely to your plans of attack.'

The patrollers moved to step inside the general store.

*   *   *

Alphonse St Cloude! Maybelle could not believe her eyes when she saw Alphonse – dressed in a fine officer's uniform – dismount from his horse in front of Troy's general store. She loitered alongside the porch with other people witnessing the gathering of the community's self-appointed leaders; she stood sideways behind a fat white woman in a flour sack dress, careful not to let Alphonse notice her in the crowd, but straining her ears to catch every word he spoke to Billy Cramer and Burt Thomas. Maybelle forced herself to remain silent when she heard the lies which Alphonse told about David and Veronica and, then, when he spoke about Posey writing letters to the North, Maybelle knew that trouble was near at hand, that she had to take word quickly back to Ham and Tim.

Maybelle, creeping through the crowd, climbed into the wagon she had left behind the store and beat the reins on the mule team to take her quickly from Troy. She first stopped at Greenleaf, jumping from the wagon, running to her husband in the stable, calling 'Ham, Ham! There's trouble! Alphonse's back! He's in cahoots with those white trash patrollers! They be ready to ride to-morrow night to Dragonard Hill like Tim's been warning us! We gots to tell Tim! We gots to go there now and tells Tim to gets ready. We gots to get ready to prepare Dragonard Hill! You be right, Ham! You and Tim be right! Those white trash patrollers are going to make trouble for Master Peter.'

'Slow down, honey,' Ham grabbed Maybelle by the arm, urging, 'Slow down and tell me this all again, slow!'

'Don't have time, Ham. Don't have time! Got to go see Tim now.' Breaking away from Ham's grip, Maybelle ran for the wagon.

Ham called, 'Tell Tim me and Bullshot will come help tonight.'

Maybelle waved goodbye and, snapping the leather reins she shouted, 'Move, you stupid mules! Move your clod-hoppers, you stupid mules!'

Maybelle did not find Tim by the stable at Dragonard Hill and, running around the main house, she dashed into the kitchen annex.

Posey glared at Maybelle from his rattan chair by the table; he snapped, 'Don't you knock, wench?'

Maybelle, near hysterics with worry, warned, 'Don't you get high-faluting with me! Where's my boy?'

'Watch your tongue, wench!' Posey said, his long fingers curling to scratch Maybelle's eyes, to pull at her headful of kinky black hair.

'Tongue? Tongue? Watch my tongue? At least I talk! I talk and don't write . . . letters!'

'What you mean, wench?' Posey demanded.

'I mean it's you – you crazy old nigger – I mean it's you who got us all in this trouble by writing those letters to Miss Veronica.'

'What you saying?'

'I'm saying none of those letters you wrote to Miss Veronica got to her! Alphonse got them! Alphonse stole them from a mailbag! He read them all! He twisted round all the facts. Now everybody says Master David and Miss Veronica and Master Peter be slave-runners!'

Posey stared blankly at Maybelle, gasping, 'Alphonse? Alphonse St Cloude got Miss Veronica's letters?'

'Yes! And he's stirring up trouble in Troy against us all!'

The announcement dazed Posey. He repeated, 'My letters, Miss Veronica never got none of my letters?'

'None! So forget about Miss Veronica. Forget about those letters! We got work to do here! Fast work! Secret work!'

Shaking his head in disbelief, Posey repeated, 'Miss

Veronica got none of my letters? That Alphonse nigger stole my letters from a mailbag?'

'I said forget about them letters, Miss Posey. You run now and check all the front windows in the big house facing the drive. Make sure the tall shutters can be bolted. We're going to need protection for shooting!'

'Shooting? What shooting?'

'Gun shooting!'

Maybelle turned and hurried from the kitchen to find Tim. Posey, still sitting alongside the table in his rattan chair, said aloud, 'Miss Veronica got none of my letters. None of the letters I done worked so hard to write . . .'

Then in a momentary flash of revenge, Posey knew what he must do. He had killed once before in his life. And now he must, once again, seek his own particular kind of revenge. Yes, Alphonse St Cloude must die.

Chapter Nineteen

FAMILIES

The adjoining downstairs parlours at Petit Jour were alive with tinkling piano music, the hubbub of voices, the occasional shrill of women's laughter; Vicky had returned from the St Charles Hotel in the afternoon and not told anyone about the accidental meeting with her son; she had forced herself to be hospitable, more gay than usual this evening, to laugh with the soldiers, teasing them that she might take part in this evening's theatricals on the top floor. General Turkel had not yet joined Vicky's nightly gathering in the parlour; she had avoided him since returning from the hotel; she knew he would ask if she had spoken to her father at the hotel, asking why Peter Abdee had come to New Orleans.

'Where is General Turkel tonight, Condesa?' asked the soldier from Pittsburgh who had portrayed one of the hunters in the recent tableau depicting lesbianism and sodomy in the wilderness.

Vicky snapped open her silk fan, joking, 'The General takes more time with his toilette than a woman! You Yankees accuse Southerners of vanity! But look! Look at all you young men!'

Flourishing her fan at the six handsome, slim-hipped young soldiers surrounding her, Vicky teased, 'Moustaches all neatly trimmed! Uniforms smartly pressed! Boots polished like mirrors!'

'Ah, but we would not be so particular about our appearance, Condesa,' said a swarthy corporal from

Buffalo, 'if we were not the guests of such a beautiful lady.'

'Flattery! How I wish it were true! But you pay me just idle flattery.'

'But it is true, Condesa!' the soldier insisted. 'We have all been discussing that very fact. We consider ourselves extremely fortunate to have made your acquaintance and, forgive the presumption, but friendship as well.'

Vicky fleetingly recalled Juanito's conduct to her, how her son was the same age as these young men, but she thought how he had spoken so disrespectfully, so insultingly to her a few hours ago in the St Charles Hotel.

Another soldier said, 'General Turkel likewise regards the Countess with great affection. He has even intimated that there might soon be plans for travel – '

'Travel!' Vicky fluttered her fan. 'You gentlemen speak as if you are all on a continental tour of Europe! Your commanding officer is no better! You do amuse me, I declare!'

The black parlour-maid, Frances, approached the small group and bent forward to whisper into Vicky's ear.

The gaiety disappeared from Vicky's face; she dropped both lace mittened hands to her lap as she listened to the maid's whispered report.

'Madame?' the corporal asked. 'Is something wrong?'

Vicky, not replying, continued to listen to the maid's whispered words; she abruptly turned to her, demanding, 'Is he here? Did he come inside the house? Is he here now?'

The corporal asked again, 'Condesa? What's the matter?'

Vicky ignored the questions; she jumped to her feet and, grabbing the maid by the arm, she shrilled, 'Damn it, Frances! Where is he? Why did you let him go?'

Shaking her head, the Negress maid pleaded, 'I just

knows what I tells you, Condesa, mam! The young man, he comes to the front door. He tells me to tell you your pappy's plantation be – '

'Silence!' Vicky hissed, pushing the maid from the parlour. 'You go follow him, you hear! You find him and tell him, ask him, even beg him to come back here! I must know exactly what he means.'

Vicky turned toward the stairs and, grabbing her long gown with one hand, she ascended the moquette covered steps in haste.

*   *   *

William Turkel offered both a military coach to be put at Vicky's immediate disposal and a search party to scan New Orleans for the young man who had brought the message to Petit Jour that Dragonard Hill was the target of local patrollers.

Vicky declined both offers; she did not want Federal soldiers to search New Orleans because she knew the caller had been Juanito, although she did not know how he even knew about the existence of Dragonard Hill. And – more astounding to her – that he knew her connection with the Abdee family.

'You are not telling me everything, Vicky,' Turkel said as he paced impatiently in front of the Oriental screen behind which Vicky was changing her clothes; she had just come upstairs from the parlour where she had earlier been entertaining the six young officers.

Vicky, anxious, distraught, disturbed by Juanito's message, replied, 'I'll explain everything to you on our way to San Francisco.'

'You mean you're finally agreeing to run away with me?'

'Run away? Hardly! You can't desert the Army, my

dear. But if we both emerge alive from the war then, yes, I'll leave New Orleans with you. But I warn you. I'll never want to return here. Once I abandon a place I'm finished with it. I have only returned to live in one place in my entire life – home – and that was a mistake.'

'Vicky, just tell me the name of the young man who came to the door.'

'Juanito . . . my son . . . Now, please, William, no more questions,' she said, emerging from behind the screen wearing breeches, tall boots and busily pinning her hair tightly against her head. 'Let's go get the horses.'

'I never underestimate your capabilities, Vicky,' Turkel said, studying her trim figure in the tight fitting clothes, 'but to ride a horse all the way to Troy?'

'I've done the trip in a carriage! I know how long it takes! I do not have time for carriages.' She looked into the mirror, smearing rouge and rice powder from her face.

'Do you know how many patrollers are in that area?'

Vicky ignored the question and asked, 'Did your men find my father at the hotel? Did they send someone to look at Chloe's house near the ramparts?'

Turkel glumly shook his head, saying, 'Your father and Chloe have both disappeared.'

'I suppose that's just as well,' she said dispassionately, pulling on a pair of tight leather gloves. 'What could Father do anyway?'

'What can you do, Vicky?' William Turkel said, standing behind her by the mirror. 'What can you and a small retinue of my men possibly achieve by racing to Dragonard Hill?'

Vicky looked at Turkel's reflection in the mirror; she said, 'William, you talk about your wife. You tell me you do not love her. That you are even going to abandon her. Yet you respect her. You keep a place for her in your heart. I have the same – what? – respect for my family. For David. For Veronica. The life I knew at Dragonard Hill. We do not choose our families. I could never again live at home. But when outsiders attack them, set out to destroy, steal from them, then, by God almighty, William, some tiny spring snaps inside you. I must go to Dragonard Hill.' She moved toward the door.

Turkel put his hand on her shoulder, trying one last time to dissuade her from the long overnight, day-long trip. 'But those patrollers. Those kind of men are a vicious, blood-hungry, cruel bunch of men. Worse than soldiers!'

'Pooh!' she said, shoving Turkel hard from her. 'I know those patrollers. Billy Cramer and those silly old geese! I'm not scared of them.'

'Then what about Alphonse St Cloude?'

Staring coldly at William Turkel, Vicky confessed, 'Nor have I forgotten about Alphonse. That is why I must go to Dragonard Hill. I know he'll do anything to be its master. I'd rather burn the place to the ground than allow that.'

*   *   *

Vicky had not ridden a horse for many years but determination made her forget discomfort; she pulled a cavalry hat further down over her face and rode alongside William Turkel, followed by his private escort toward the Pontchartrain Road which led north; Vicky tried to put all thoughts of Juanito from her mind; she tried not to fathom the reasons he had come tonight to Petit Jour and left a message for her about Dragonard Hill; she wondered nonetheless if Juanito now knew he had Abdee blood in his veins intermixed with the blood of the arrogant Veradaga family. If so, who had told

212

him? Had his visit tonight to the house been a token gesture of loyalty to his mother, the maternal side of his family? Vicky smiled to herself as she galloped along the dirt road in the moonlight; she could not claim friendship with her son but she knew – remembering his father – that a strict form of etiquette, of politeness, of loyalty was imbued in him . . . and it came not only from his Veradaga blood. Juanito had come to her, helping her to save Dragonard Hill, because he also was an Abdee.

*　　*　　*

The light from the same moon glistened across the gulf stream, illuminating the full white sails of the *Pina;* Juan Carlos and his captain took turns at the wheel, letting the ship luff, tightening the sails to breaking point against the growing wind, conning a course toward the Florida Straits and then home to Havana. Home. Juanito thought about leaving New Orleans, about Petit Jour, about his mother, about the Abdee family. He now realized that the old English slave-dealer in Regla, Richard Abdee, had sent him to America to make some contact with his past, his family, and Juanito stood behind the ship's wheel, wondering if he would seek out the old Englishman on his return to Havana. No. He decided. 'I think not. Richard Abdee and his black mistress with the burned face can solve their own riddles. I met my mother. I have done my duty to her family. I shall now be my own man. Not my father's son. Not an Abdee heir. But me. Juanito. Nothing more. I also will call myself "Tomorrow".'

*　　*　　*

The Justice of the Peace stood in front of Peter Abdee and Chloe St Cloude; he held a bible in his chapped hands; a candle flickered inside the small Missouri sod house, lighting the tired faces of a woman dressed in a ragged robe and a gangly, one-legged boy leaning on a wooden crutch; they were the witnesses for Peter and Chloe in their simple wedding ceremony.

'Chloe Marie St Cloude, do you take Peter Abdee to be your lawfully wedded husband?'

'I do,' she murmured.

'Peter Abdee, do you take this woman, Chloe Marie St Cloude, to be your lawfully wedded wife?'

Peter smiled in the candlelight, happily responding, 'Third time's the charm!'

The statement jolted the Justice of the Peace; he frowned at Peter.

But Peter could not hide his happy, even coltish feelings; he was at long last marrying Chloe; he had decided to strike out in the world, to snatch the last chance of freedom in some far and still undecided place, a land not worked by slaves, a country not inherited nor foisted upon him by family nor in-laws; Peter was in love, happy, free at last to enjoy his own life; he had worked to free other people around him; now he could concentrate on his own freedom.

He replied, 'I do.'

*   *   *

Loraine Cramer lay curled alone on a corncob mattress as she listened to her husband return to their cabin from another meeting with the patrollers of Carterville and Troy; she had carefully washed herself to remove all traces of Sebbie's musty smell but she still worried that Billy might detect some odour, a kinky black hair, any

214

telltale sign which would betray that she was the mistress of a black slave from Greenleaf Plantation.

Cramer's voice boomed across the room lit only by a taper flickering in a bowl of bear fat. 'We're going to get the sons-of-bitches this time. We're going to wipe Peter Abdee's and his God-damned niggers' noses in the dirt.'

Loraine knew that her husband had been drinking with the patrollers; she also had become aware that the patrollers were planning an attack tomorrow night, some form of a ride-of-revenge which she did not thoroughly understand; she was concerned only with her passion for young Sebbie.

'Oh, Lord,' she prayed to herself as she lay curled on the crude mattress, 'I'm not asking for no favours for myself. Just make that young Sebbie buck safe. He's been mighty good to me. Maybe not what saints would call goodness, Lord. But to a lonely body like me, living with a mean devil like Billy Cramer, that Sebbie buck has been an angel to me. So, Lord, if anybody gets punished for wrong-doings, don't make it Sebbie. Whatever happens in the future, Lord, punish wicked selfish people like Billy. Even me if I be wrong and sinful. Lord, my love-making with Sebbie might not be righteous and proper. But if it weren't for getting to know Sebbie in that way, Lord Jesus, I'd never know that black folks ain't as bad as white people say. So protect them, Lord, against the mean ones of us. Thank you, Lord. Amen.' Then Loraine Cramer tried to sleep as her husband continued to rant across the small cabin, cursing Peter Abdee, Dragonard Hill, Greenleaf, and 'niggers'.

Chapter Twenty

A GRANDMOTHER'S STORY

'Niggers! Step to it!'

Maybelle hurried the field slaves from town into the back door of Dragonard Hill, ignoring the black people's trepidation about coming into the big house, about entering territory forbidden to them.

Bare feet padded across parquet floors and silk carpets; the slaves moved quickly, quietly, orderly; Maybelle had worked all last night and all today choosing the men and women from town, selecting only the people whom she knew genuinely recognized what Peter Abdee had been doing for them, slaves who realized that their new cabins and plots of ground were steps towards emancipation, towards a life as human beings.

Tim, Ham and Bullshot had arranged muskets, pistols and rifles by each of the front windows; they piled ammunition at regular intervals between them.

Ham, waiting until Maybelle had finished leading the black recruits to the artillery and ammunition posts in the parlour and dining-room, told Tim that he now was going outside to make last minute checks on other slaves he had stationed in the darkness of shrubberies and trees, positions flanking the driveway which climbed the hill from the public road.

Posey stood in one corner of the main hallway, soberly watching the rough field slaves trampling into the house he had guarded all his life as if it were a sacred shrine; Posey was not angered by the intrusion, did not dwell on the fact that these were changing times; he kept the kitchen girl from Greenleaf by his side; Posey knew that Hettie was ambitious and he had struck his own bargain with her; Posey held manumission papers folded in one hand; Posey could read and write, could forge manumission papers which would free Hettie immediately from slavery; Hettie stood obediently alongside Posey, willing to perform the one task he had asked her to do, already wearing the Confederate flag wrapped around her naked body, even anticipating helping Posey seek his revenge and, then, she could escape forever from Dragonard Hill, be a free woman of colour with papers to prove it.

*   *   *

The patrollers collected in darkness at the foot of the hill, men from Carterville and Troy grouping under trees by the graveyard to avoid detection in the moonlight.

'The main house looks empty,' Alphonse observed, sitting on his horse, staring up the hill and seeing no lights flickering between the six Doric columns of Dragonard Hill.

Burt Thomas sat on a dappled mare alongside Alphonse; he grumbled, 'I still think we should ride straight to the slave quarters. Put a torch to those shacks. Tie ropes around all the niggers' necks. Cart them straight to the Grouse Place.'

Alphonse disagreed. 'The main house is a symbol to the slaves. To the whole neighbourhood. Once we take possession of the main house, the rest will be easy.'

'Burn the damned place down,' Thomas grumbled. 'That's what we should do. Put a torch to the whole works. That'll show Abolitionist trash!'

'No fire!' Alphonse warned.

Chad Tucker, cantering towards Alphonse from the

far end of the grouped patrollers, called, 'The boys from Carterville are all here now.'

'Shush!' Thomas nodded toward the graveyard behind them. 'Want to wake up the dead, big mouth!'

Tombstones and wooden grave markers shimmered in the moonlight inside the picket fence; two white granite angels guarded the graves of the two women, Melissa Selby and Kate Breslin, who had been the wives of Peter Abdee and bore him his heirs.

Cramer frowned at Thomas and, then, he unfurled a leather whip from his saddle horn; he snapped the whip and rode toward the stone pillars supporting the cast iron words – *Dragonard Hill*.

Men mounted on horses and mules moved forward – a small army of more than four dozen shabbily-dressed men; Cramer passed between the pillars, the first to ride up the road leading to the house.

Alphonse, realizing that Billy Cramer and Burt Thomas were still competing for leadership, knew that he must prevent them from arguing and putting a torch to the house; they could seize part of the slave population but he had to claim command of Dragonard Hill tonight or forget his ambitions forever of becoming its master.

The patrollers from Troy and Carterville proceeded in groups toward the gates; they passed under the iron arc, the first riders now galloping up the hill.

The last man on horseback had barely passed under the arc when two figures rushed from the trees flanking the gate posts and hurriedly shut the creaking gates.

'Niggers!'

Ham and six more men stepped from the trees; they fired on the patroller as he raised his squirrel gun.

'There, too!' shouted another patroller, pointing toward movement in the cypress trees lining the driveway. 'More niggers!'

'They got guns!'

'A trap!'

'Don't panic!' shouted Alphonse, pulling out his pistol; he ordered, 'Ride up the hill. Take cover by the main house!'

But when the first of the patrol column reached the top of the incline, more black slaves stepped from behind the six Doric columns; the night exploded with red and yellow charges as the Negroes fired at the patrollers.

'Split!' shouted Alphonse, waving the Carterville men to one side, trying to organize men armed only with whips, knives, clubs, all crude weapons.

Burt Thomas was the first patroller to be struck by a musket ball; men scattered when they saw blood spurt from his chest.

Cramer, excited by action, shouted to his followers, 'Make torches! Burn the son-of-a-bitching place to the ground!'

'No!' Alphonse cried. 'No fire!'

Ignoring Alphonse, Cramer insisted, 'Put everything to the torch!'

But then another round of gunshot fired from inside the house; Cramer's men retreated towards the trees; Cramer struck one match, then a second in the safety of a chinaberry copse.

Alphonse shouted, 'God damn it, Cramer! Don't burn the house!'

A voice then called to him, 'St Cloude? Alphonse St Cloude?'

Alphonse looked toward the side of the house; he did not at first believe his eyes. But, yes, it was Hettie, the kitchen girl from Greenleaf.

She beckoned him towards her.

Alphonse looked closely and saw Hettie was wrapped in a flag, a Confederate flag.

She called, 'I'm with you! I'm on . . . your side!'

Alphonse remembered how ambitious she was; he believed he understood her intention when she beckoned him toward the kitchen annex.

Then Alphonse looked from Hettie to Cramer who was lighting a pine torch; Alphonse raised his pistol, aimed at Cramer, pulled the trigger, felled him with one fatal shot.

It was when Alphonse jumped off his horse and dashed toward Hettie that Ham led his group of Negroes up the hill, blocking all the patrollers trying to escape down to the public road.

Clubs. Squirrel guns. Knives. The patrollers' weapons were useless against the ammunition of the black men. Nor did their passion match that of the slaves.

White men fell to the ground. Black men, emboldened by a taste of victory, attacked patrollers with their bare hands, pulling them from their horses and mules, overcoming them with fists and clenched fingers.

The gun-fire subsided in the house; the front doors opened; Tim, rushing between the columns, saw the carnage and he shouted, 'Stop! We've won! We've done enough! We've won!'

The killing, the beating, the slaughter continued; the black slaves showed no mercy for the patrollers who wanted to lock them in pens, paid no heed to men begging for their lives, half-dead people desperately pleading to live, making promises for future equality.

Maybelle stood alongside Tim; she said, 'Boy, you just start thinking now how we gets our folks back to their houses. They'll stop soon. Nobody wants to go on killing for ever.'

Tim continued staring at the spectacle, black men finally achieving domination over white. Was it worth it? Was any protection of guns worth this amount of killing?

Maybelle repeated her maternal advice, 'Boy, you just start thinking about how we gets our folks back to their houses. We've got to gets rid of these guns, too. Niggers ain't meant to have guns. Not if we want a peaceful future. We've gots to clean away every trace we was here before snoopers come. So, boy, hop to it!'

Tim – tired, disillusioned, sad – squeezed his corpulent mother, asking, 'Shall I gets Pa to help me?'

'Hells bells, yes, boy! That's what a family's for! Nigger or white. To helps.' She stepped forward to look for Ham herself.

*   *   *

The sky was lighting dawn blue as the small escort of Federal soldiers moved slowly up the hill from the public road.

Bodies of dead white men littered the driveway, corpses smeared with blood, throats gashed from ear to ear, stomachs slashed open, genitals sliced from groins, swarms of flies already covering the bodies like iridescent robes.

General Turkel's voice was flat. 'A battlefield. Another God-damned battlefield.'

Vicky remained silent, riding slowly toward the front pillars of Dragonard Hill.

Turkel looked at men's chests exploded by cartridges, foreheads pierced by bullets, stomachs gouged with bayonets. He asked, 'Where do the slaves live?'

Vicky nodded toward the east. 'Their quarter is beyond that hill.'

Turkel shook his head in bewilderment. 'Look at what these poor white sons-of-bitches were fighting with! Like savages!'

Vicky asked, 'Who do you think did this?'

'Renegade Confederates. Yankees.' Turkel took a deep sigh. 'This is war time. Who knows? Except that it wasn't slaves. Look at what these men had to defend themselves with. Crude, the most crude weapons I've ever seen. And if white men only had these, a slave could certainly not get better. No, it had to be . . . who knows?'

'The front doors look locked,' Vicky said. 'Let's see if there's any life around back.'

'Be careful,' Turkel called.

'It's only the kitchen annex out back,' Vicky shouted, cantering over the lawn.

*　　　*　　　*

Vicky and General Turkel stood side by side in the doorway to the kitchen annex; they stared in silence at Posey busily working at the kitchen table.

Posey, too involved in his early morning chore, did not greet them; he moved quickly around the kitchen table, placing saucers, plates and small bowls on the table to catch blood pouring from the naked corpse of Alphonse St Cloude. Posey jabbered as he worked.

'Nigger blood! See! Nothing but black nigger blood.' Posey collected the bowls from the arteries he had opened on the naked body, replacing them with empty saucers to catch more blood flowing fresh, warm, almost black from the veins. 'Alphonse St Cloude ain't got white blood in his veins. He's a nigger. Nothing but common trash nigger.'

'Mad,' Turkel whispered, 'that person's . . . insane.'

Ignoring Turkel, Vicky softly called, 'Posey, remember me? It's Vicky.'

Posey continued moving the saucers and bowls. 'I be with you in a jiffy, Miss Vicky and Miss Veronica. I just gots to finish this job to show to Master Peter. To show

222

everybody that Alphonse St Cloude ain't nothing but a nigger.'

'What happened here, Miss Posey?' Vicky quietly asked.

'Happened? You wants to know what happened? Ask Master Peter. I'm just be a nigger. I don't know nothing.'

Turkel said, 'The guns. Who shot the patrollers with the guns?'

'Guns? What guns? The soldiers came and took all the guns.'

Vicky pressed, 'But what happened, Miss Posey? There are bodies all over the driveway. Who killed them? Who had the guns?'

'Guns? What do I know about guns? I'm just a nigger . . . an old nigger granny . . . gots three grand-children living in Boston . . .'

Posey hurried to set a crockery bowl beneath Alphonse's jawbone, replacing a blue willow-patterned saucer brimming with dark blood still trickling from a knife gash in his neck.

Vicky began to speak again, to ask Posey about the killings, but she realized that Posey – and probably no other black slave either here or at Greenleaf – would ever confide about the battle, the slaughter, the *Guns of Dragonard*.